SOMETHING DISGUISED

T.R. Kester

Contents:

SOMETHING DISGUISED

Copyright © 2019 by TR Kester

DEDICATION

For Melissa, my sister, who taught me that our vulnerabilities' are our strengths.

For Susan & Robyn, who I adore, love and value more than they'll ever know.

For Maria, my Queen of Good Magic and who embodies all that is beautiful in the world.

For Neil, who I love unconditionally.

For Kimmy, who is both brave and bold.

"We are so accustomed to disguise ourselves to others, that in the end, we become disguised to ourselves."

—**François de La Rochefoucauld**

CHARACTERS

Pogue Witches:

Aaron

Noah

Perry

Bermuda

Isadora

Shane

Romani Coven:

Pilar

Madelyn

Addison

Dantalian

Persia

Brady

Extended Family:

Ravenna - *Wife of Aaron Pogue*

Connemara Penthal - *Wife of Noah Pogue*

Kathryn Penthal - *Sister of Connemara*

Andromeda Pogue (New) - *The twin sister of Bermuda, resides in Vancouver, Canada*

Mars Romani (New) - *Twin brother of Persia and Dantalian*

Serene Rein - *Step-daughter of Pilar and elf Queen of the Autumn Forest.*

Owen & Lyndon - *Isadora's twin sons*

Johdi Fox - *Pogue Cousin, father's side of the family and an Omega Witch*

Juliann, Siobhan and Zane - *members of the Romani Triad, siblings of Pilar Romani*

Good Witches, Romani & Good Magical Beings:

Philomena Beaumont - *Ancestor. Sister of Tempest, Great Aunt of Aaron, Noah and Perry Pogue*

Nathaniel Eames - *Pogue Ancestor from Colonial Salem*

(Kalena) Pridham - *A female Custodian appointed to the Pogue Family (was a witch in her past life in Ancient Babylon)*

Aryan - *A Mongkukulam (Filipino witch) who came to be possessed by the Old One, Vesta*

Esmeralda D'hôte - *Romani Ancestor during Ancient Babylon*

Judea, Inara and Nera - *Romani Ancestors during Ancient Babylon, sister's of Esmeralda*

Uphara - *Pogue Ancestor, powerful sorceress during Ancient Egypt and maid of Cleopatra*

Pluto, Venus, Saturn and Mars - *Planetary deities, respectfully the past lives of Noah, Perry and Aaron Pogue. Saturn, the only female remains unidentified.*

Atropos - *The power, ruler over the Gods of Witchcraft and a sister of fate, also one of three Original Witches*

Lindsay Hogue - *Pogue Ancestor and powerful witch during Ancient Babylon, daughter of Uphara*

Renae Ketch - *A female Custodian appointed to Pilar Romani and family*

Grace Leighton - *Princess of the Dragons, Ancient Babylon*

Beastial - *term used for a celestial creatures, like Dragons, Griffins etc*

Säde - *A powerful witch during Ancient Babylon, has the power of Cyrokinesis*

Spectra - *Goddess of the Stars*

Rathe - *An Old One*

Deific - *Associated guardian of a Hellmouth*

Evelina - *Weather Sprite/Tempo Being, Supercell Storm*

Estia Bradmore - *Clairvoyant Medium who purchases Aaron Pogue's home*

Alessia - *Woodland Fairy*

Daniela - *Woodland Fairy*

Demons & Evil Beings:

Rafaela - *Evil Demigoddess, and Whore of Babylon*

Melpomene - *The Muse of Tragedy and seized control over Limbo*

The Enthusa - *Melpomene's muse underlings*

Pelasgus - *Perry Pogue's vampire name*

Asmodeus - *An ancient demon king. Entombed in ice by the goddess, Rhea*

The Duodecim - *Twelve Demon Disciples, they are the polar opposite of the ones that followed Jesus and believed to the ultimate controllers of the Underworld.*

Alera - *An evil witch and powerful force during Ancient Babylon*

Callidora - *An evil witch during Ancient Babylon and past life of Connemara Penthal*

Kailash - *An evil witch during Ancient Babylon, sister of Callidora*

Cissy - *An evil witch during Ancient Babylon, sister of Callidora & Kailash*

Kasi - *An Oracle in Ancient Babylon*

Kamenwati/Kamen - *Powerful Nightmare Soldier & Rafaela's right-hand demon*

Dark Promise Coven - *A congregation of evil witches that follows Alera.* _The Judges - *Evil witches turned into demons as a reward for their worship to Asmodeus*

Lazarus - *King of the Vampires during Ancient Babylon*

Asterix - *Dark Fairy*

INSPIRED TRAGEDY

*T*he world was miserable, dull with a gray, almost rainy sky and opposite to the world of the living which was full of color and life. In the highest point in the sky, two points rippled like water and two golden orbs entered Limbo. They fell like comets to the earth below with shiny, golden tails. Beneath the cloud mass, steady rain fell. Touching the ground, the golden orbs rose abruptly and took on human forms. They were beautiful and blonde- Bermuda and Andromeda. Confused a little, they turned their heads and scanned their new surroundings. A forest of towering and imposing trees, it had that same eerie feeling like a scene from a horror movie where the innocent woman, alone on the road would succumb to the beast which lurked in the shadows.

"Where are we?" Andromeda queried curiously.

Bermuda turned about on the spot. "Is this Limbo?" Peering ahead through the fog, she made out faint outlines of buildings. "I think there is a town ahead of us."

Extending her arms out in front, Andromeda tried to use her power of Energy Manipulation. And lucky for her, it worked. Magically, her power expelled the fog and a colonial town emerged.

"What?" Andromeda murmured with confusion as she lowered her arms. "What the hell? I don't like this place already and we've only just got here."

In a ripple of energy, Pilar manifested. "Keep your guard up. Call for me when you are ready to return to your bodies. I will be acting as your anchor." In another ripple of energy, she was gone.

A figure slipped from the forest behind the two witches as they focused their attention on the town ahead of them. They were completely unaware of the presence.

Melpomene was beautiful and poised, just as you would imagine something otherworldly to be and true to the definition of a Muse. But beneath the radiance was a calculating evil. Venturing up behind Andromeda, she breathed against the skin of the witch's neck as she used her power of Inspiration.

"You don't want to save them..." Her lips almost kissed the witch. "...leave them here. Let them move on to the afterlife. Death is easier."

Andromeda moved uneasily as she succumbed to the enchantress' magic. "Perhaps we're making a mistake being here," she doubted herself. "Maybe this is what is best- letting Noah and Perry move on."

Placing her hand on her sister's arm, Bermuda destroyed Melpomene's influence and together they headed down the dirt road. Repelled backward by Pogue magic, the Muse abruptly halted, hissed irritably and in a fluttering wind her long teal hair blew about before she disappeared in a glow.

The two sisters walked cautiously down the middle of the gravel road toward the colonial town. It consisted of wooden buildings, shops, saloons and a church with a great steeple.

~*~

Inside the protective circle in the real world– Pilar, Bermuda and Andromeda stood entranced as they traveled to another dimension.

Perry slowly sat up as if he was possessed. For a long moment he sat motionless, staring ahead at nothing.

A curious Isadora observed him.

Turning his head slightly, Aaron focused on Philomena as she stood directly behind Pilar but on the outside of the circle. Fiddling with the pink crystal in his hand, he murmured an incantation.

"Rest state, Stone mate, I return you to heaven's gate."

Feeling as though she was being pulled back, Philomena let out a gasp. Her spirit was whisked back to heaven and her body turned to stone. Aaron, the mortal, had successfully banished the powerful Gamma Witch from the house. Stalking around the room, he halted behind her, elevated his leg and kicked the stone figure in the back; destroying it.

Startled, Isadora gasped in fright. She wasn't sure what was happening and was confused as to why Aaron would do that to his own ancestor?

"What the hell are you doing?" She covered her mouth in horror. "Why would you do that?" Turning her head, her attention became focused on the stirring body in the circle. "Perry?" she murmured cautiously, hoping he would bring some kind of solution.

Using his vampire ability of Accelerated Movement, Perry rose to his feet and slammed against an invisible barrier which kept him within the circle. The whole idea of a Spirit Prison was to hold a summoned spirit or prevent evil escaping it. In irritation his face morphed and he assumed his vampire visage. Behind him, his body lay on the floor alongside Noah.

Perry remained unconscious, so this version of him; standing and breathing was his vampire personality, Pelasgus. Caydit Packrem's artiste, as she would call him. He calmed himself, closed his eyes and inhaled.

"Kill them!" Aaron, growled in a foreign female voice, "Pelasgus!"

Isadora's eyebrows rose and she tilted her head, startled by both voice and words. "Wait! What? Why would you say that?"

Spontaneously, Pelasgus' eyes opened and with a sharp exhale he blew out the flames dancing atop the candles. The magical barrier keeping him contained within the circle was suddenly insufficient. He stepped over the candles and halted. Isadora and he exchanged different stares– her's was fearful and his, well... murderous!

Aaron stood poised behind the circle, almost behind Pilar, "KILL THEM NOW!!"

Perry, otherwise known as Pelasgus' vampire visage, was intimidating and utilizing his Accelerated Movement ability. He shot toward her as she proceeded to step in front of Shane. As her hungry vampire uncle came within metres of her, Isadora elevated her arm and struck forwards with a fierce look in her eyes. Her fist ignited with a subtle glow and she opened her hand, activating her power of Photokinesis, generating a vibrant blast of energy and light.

With an outcry of pain, Pelasgus was sent flying across the room with impressive force and slammed against the wall. Falling toward the floor, he flicked his head up and glared at Isadora from across the room before vanishing in a speeding blur.

"Shane," Isadora began, turning her head to address the male over her shoulder as she lowered her arm, "I need you to be competent. I don't give a shit about confident, just–"

Out of nowhere, Pelasgus reappeared in front of Isadora.

Reacting, she mentally wielded her power of Energy Manipulation and his clenched fist slammed against an invisible barrier which rippled upon his impact. "And you thought I had let my guard down, didn't you moron?" They exchanged sinister glares. "I could sense your movement by feeling the energy in the room." Using brisk hand gestures, she blasted him with energy, catapulting him backward into the table, breaking it and sending the table's contents all over the floor. "You might be faster, but I am stronger."

~*~

*O*bserving the grey sky, Bermuda pondered her own

mortality... was this what people experienced when passing from living to deceased? It was cold and hardly what one could call Paradise. Lowering her head, she observed the wooden buildings as they ambled along the town's cobbled streets. The people around them were ghosts clad in colonial clothing. Women wore tailored dresses with bonnets; the men wore suits, some with top hats.

"This place is freaking weird," Andromeda murmured. "I dare say this is Salem Massachusetts." Fascinated, she observed her surroundings.

The two sister witches were dressed in a more to-date, twenty-first century attire.

Negotiating the busy street, they approached the town center square where there was a pyre, and a man stood tied to a wooden stake with his head hung. Observing him from afar,

Bermuda immediately recognized the victim by his jeans and western-style shirt as well as his shaggy brown mop of hair- Noah Pogue.

"Andy." She pointed toward him. "Look, its Noah. Over there, tied to that stake."

Acknowledging the individual, a grim expression crossed Andromeda's face, she brushed her long blonde hair away from her face. There was a hint of hope in her eyes.

"Oh God."

They pushed their way through the crowd. Behind them, in their wake, a beautiful woman stood- Melpomene dressed in a beautiful and ethereal gown. Swaying her arm up and out in front of her, she pointed her finger at Noah.

"Conceal!" she commanded.

The second individual tied to the wooden stake behind Noah faded out of sight as Bermuda and Andromeda came to the foot of the pyre.

Turning around, Melpomene admired the steeple of the church and again, elevated her arm, pointed at the window ledge and used her magic.

"Reveal!" she commanded.

A vision of a bound Perry manifested with glittering teal magic on the ledge. "Welcome." She turned her head and glanced over her shoulder at the twin sister witches. "To my playground. My game. My rules." She then vanished in a teal glow.

Climbing up onto the mound, Bermuda untied Noah's hands from behind the stake and his legs. His exhausted body fell forward. Andromeda, below, raised her hand and used her power of Energy Manipulation to hold him in place and prevent him from falling to the ground.

"Help him down, Bermuda," she instructed.

Bermuda's long hair covered half her face as she gave her sister a cold glare, "Don't help me or anything, I'll do it my fricken self."

Noah murmured, "Perry..." his throat dry and voice stricken, "help, Perry."

Bermuda flicked her hair away from her face as she helped her uncle down onto the ground. "I-I," she appeared puzzled; "I swear I saw someone else tied to the stake with Noah."

"You know what thought did," Andromeda retorted sarcastically as she observed the wooden stake. "But I did think the same as we got closer."

An inspired voice whispered through her mind. "Way up high is where the birds fly." Andromeda looked up but saw no birds.

An invisible Melpomene stepped around the witch. "The faithful kind too, send their prayers so high." Turning around, she inspected the weatherboard church at street level and lifted her eyes as she traced the structure, halting them on window ledge of the steeple. "He believes he can fly."

Gasping, Andromeda acknowledged the male, "Perry!"

"What?" Bermuda asked as she sat Noah down on the ground. "Where do you...." Standing, she turned and noticed her sister's absence. "Andy?"

Below her, Noah groaned with discomfort. "You're a Custodian. Can't you like...." She waved her hands in the air. "....heal yourself or something?" He groaned again, tipping over and laying on his side. "Oh, for god's sake." She brushed her hair back irritably and sat him back upright. "Here." She placed her hand inside his. "Take my hand. I'm channeling the Hellmouth then my magic is amplified." She had an idea. Placing his hand against her heart, she closed her eyes and placed her free hand over his forehead. "Flow from he." Opening her eyes, the power of the Hellmouth was evident by the pure blue energy consuming her eyes. "Into me, *power move fluent and free. I call upon his power to heal, through my hand. I will command."*

Suddenly, with her spell, a golden glow flowed through Noah's arm and into his hand. Passing through into Bermuda, the glow moved up her arm and her hand upon his forehead gave off a brilliant shine. The glow consumed Noah's entire body. Gasping, he felt himself revitalized and when the aura faded, his grazes and rough-looking appearance was restored to a more humble look.

"Bermuda...." His hypnotizing sapphire blue eyes glimmered with emotion. "Oh, thank God." He lunged forward and wrapped his arms around her as she lowered her arms back to her side. "I thought we'd die here."

Bermuda pulled away. "We, what do you mean?" They exchanged odd looks. "Where is Perry?"

Rising to his feet, Noah turned and pointed out Perry who had been standing behind him, tied to the wooden stake the entire time.

A puzzled Bermuda pointed at the male and touched her mouth in a moment of quiet confusion.

"What the hell? He wasn't there before." Spinning around, she looked about the busy town square to see if she could point out her sister Andromeda by her modern attire. "Who the hell did Andy see? She said Perry's name and ran off."

"Help," Noah called out from on top of the pyre, "Help me untie him so I can heal him."

Bermuda sprinted up the mount and began assisting her uncle.

"What do you know about Limbo, Bermuda?"

Pausing for a moment, she gazed at him with uncertainty. "Not a lot."

"This world is supposed to be beautiful and inviting. A place where the deceased travel to get to the other side, but I fear evil has made its claim here."

Bermuda asked, "What kind of evil?"

"Rafaela. This dimension is governed by Melpomene," Noah said.

"Melpomene? As in the Muse Queen of Tragedy?" Turning away, she summoned in a loud voice, "Pilar!"

Pilar manifested in a glow. "Bermuda?"

"Pilar, what does the Book of Shadows say about Melpomene? She is one of the nine Muse Queens and Inspirer of Tragedy, is she not?"

Pilar closed her eyes for a moment.

In the real world, flames ignited atop the white candles which created the protective circle. The pages of the Pogue Book of Shadows flipped in a magical wind and then fell flat on the pages marked: The Nine Muse Queens.

"It says," Pilar to began to read the pages with her power of telepathy. "Melpomene is the most beautiful and powerful of the Nine Muse Queens and daughters of Zeus and Mnemosyne. She governs Limbo. The Enthusa, Melpomene's muses linger about the dimension, assisting souls who get lost instead of crossing over." Glancing over her shoulder, the disturbance in the real world, in Aaron Pogue's attic drew her attention, "Something isn't right here. Hurry. Don't get separated. Stay together. Melpomene might attempt to kill you if Noah thinks the dimension has become tainted."

Untying Perry, his body fell against Noah and he almost lost his balance.

"I see you," said an egotistical voice from below. "Witch!"

Bermuda turned and acknowledged the woman in black. "Clever of you to see through the Queen's magic, but it's a pity for

18

your sister." The woman's humble appearance quickly morphed. Her eyes sank and became grey with heavy black shadow around them and her beautiful lips turned charcoal with black shadowing. "You will not get out alive."

"She's an Enthusa?" Bermuda asked softly and Noah nodded his head. "Great, heal him and I'll deal with the Black Widow." Jumping from the pyre, she landed on her feet directly in front of the evil muse. "So, how are we going to do this?"

The woman reached her arm back and then forwards as she attempted to strike. With a brilliant flash of gold energy, the creature struck Bermuda's power of Deflection and was catapulted backwards with impressive force.

"What the hell power, was that?" Noah called out in shock.

Bermuda's eyes refilled with the blue energy of the Hellmouth as she smirked. "Hellmouth Power." Her voice sounded deep and intimidating.

"You what?" Noah blurted out in a high-pitched voice. You're not strong enough. It's too strong, it will kill you."

She looked at him over her shoulder, "Watch me."

Across the town square, inside the church, Andromeda paused as she took in its regal interior. Behind her the heavy doors closed with a clunk. Cautiously, she moved down the center aisle.

In her shadow, Melpomene appeared dressed in her beautiful teal Grecian gown. Her eyes glittered with power and her curled smile revealed her wickedness.

Halting, Andromeda looked up at the ceiling, pondering the way to the steeple so she could rescue Perry. From the corner of her eye, something teal in color caught her attention.

"You're a pretty witch!" Melpomene cooed.

Andromeda was struck by a blast of teal colored energy and launched backwards down the aisle. Hitting the steps of the altar, she let out a cry of pain before she crashed onto the ground.

Shrugging off the attack, Andromeda- aided by the power of the Hellmouth, evident by the blue energy in her eyes– levitated back onto her feet.

Letting out a cry, she pushed both her arms out in front of her and projected a powerful wave of telekinetic energy. Like her sister, Isadora, she could also manipulate energy. The wooden church pews were obliterated and thrown backwards. The rubble blocked the doorway of the church so no one was able to enter.

"I've met Glinda the Good Witch." Melpomene spoke sarcastically. "It's a pity you can't hold a candle to her. We all know about your coming, the great and powerful Pogue Witches."

Andromeda lowered her arms. "I suppose you also heard about getting your ass kicked?"

Accelerating forwards in a blur, Melpomene abruptly halted in front of the witch. "No." She smirked and moved her arm at her side. "But I heard you were going to die."

Letting out a cry, "BERMUDA!" and hunching forwards, Andromeda felt the hot metal of a knife penetrate her abdomen. "...help me."

Pulling her weapon free of the witch's body, Melpomene watched her victim stagger for a moment, clutching her mortal wound before falling to the ground.

"Not all dogs go to heaven," Melpomene chuckled. "And not all good witches. You don't come into my dimension and try what doesn't belong to you."

CHAPTER TWO

INSPIRED TRAGEDY – PART TWO

*O*n the floor of the church, Andromeda lay lifeless as the shimmer of life within quickly faded. Melpomene stood proud of her accomplishment; she'd successfully killed a Pogue Witch. Behind her, individual masses of black smoke wafted down from the ceiling and upon landing on the floor, four Enthusa appeared, so beautiful, so inspiring.

"My queen," the one on the far right acknowledged. "What an inspiration you are, killing a Pogue Witch is a feat no one has ever achieved before."

The Muse Queen smirked confidently. "I am not just anyone." Emitting an ear-piercing scream, the Enthusa was vanquished and her body exploded into black smoke which quickly disappeared. "Let this be a reminder to the rest of you- I am Melpomene, Muse of Tragedy." Folding her arms across her chest and now appearing smug, she instructed, "Place the body in the cell beside Aaron Pogue." The Enthusa moved forward, gathering around Andromeda.

~*~

*O*utside in the town square, Bermuda engaged the Enthusa. She flipped backwards and upon landing on her feet, she leapt into the air and kicked the woman in the torso, causing her to stagger backwards. Straightening up, the being of inspiration extended her arm forwards and threw a blue sparkling ball of energy at the witch. Lifting her hand, Bermuda deflected it with her power, creating a golden glow which encompassed her entire hand. Letting out a scream, the Enthusa was struck with her own power and exploded into a cloud of black smoke.

"Now that's inspiration," Bermuda remarked nastily. On feeling an excruciating pain in her abdomen, she let out a scream of pain and dropped to her hands and knees. "Oh God, what's happening?" Turning her head, she observed a healed Perry climbing to his feet as Noah approached her. Her hearing became inaudible, her vision blurry. "I feel like I'm dying..." She collapsed onto the ground, whispering, "Andromeda."

A frantic Noah dropped to his knees, turned Bermuda's lifeless body onto her back and noted the bloody wound in her abdomen which was laced with the glittering magic of inspiration. As a side-effect of combining their magic and drawing on their power as twins, they had both succumbed to the same fate. It was an inspired death.

"Bermuda!" Noah shook her. "Come on Bermuda, wake up for me. Come on."

Hurrying to his brother's side, Perry paused, a grim expression on his face. Peering up, Noah's emotional eyes met his brother's, a million and one questions within them, but not one conclusion.

"Go! Find Andromeda. now, Perry." His voice was deep as he growled at Perry before crying out as a tear fled the corner of his eye. "Pilar, I need you!"

Perry left and hurried to the church. He hesitated at the door, turning and looking himself over when he realized he wasn't able to move with acceleration. Then, he noted he could not assume his vampire visage. Elevating his hands, he turned them over and began pondering what was wrong. Looking ahead, he showed a *bold confidence and used his power of Telekinesis to open the doors and enter.*

~*~

Reaching his feet in an accelerated blur, Pelasgus grinned at Isadora with hungry eyes. A deep animal growl emerged from his chest and he moved toward her.

"Isolate." With a brisk swing of her arm, she cast a spell and he stopped in his tracks. The bones in his body stiffened as his entire skeletal structure made cracking noises. "Now dislocate."

He felt his bones break and cried out in pain.

"Suffer, you evil son of a–"

She was cut off midsentence by a woman's voice from behind her.

"Isadora," summoned Ravenna.

Isadora spun around and was greeted by Shane.

"You're a good girl." The dark haired woman dropped the boy's body to the floor, revealing a swirly blade Athame she had used to stab him in the back. "Now surrender or die."

An outraged Isadora took a step backward, "Go to hell you pitiful bit–" she began to raise her hand.

"How dare you raise your hand at your mother." Ravenna snarled and using her power of Telekinesis, she launched Isadora backwards into the air. "I gave you life, you miserable insect."

Isadora crashed against the invisible barrier of the protection circle, causing it to flash and then fell onto the floor. Trying to dismiss the pain in her body, she reached towards Pelasgus and used the power of Energy Manipulation on him.

"Dislocate."

Letting out a pain-stricken roar, Pelasgus buckled to his knees as his bones broke.

Pulling herself from the floor, Isadora acknowledged a deceased Shane at Ravenna's feet. She felt her body shaking with fear, but kept a cool, calm and collected demeanor about her.

"You are no mother of mine. Who the hell are you?" She aimed a look of revulsion towards Ravenna. "I should have listened to Bermuda when she said your thoughts were disturbing." To her right, just out of her peripheral vision, Aaron began to move towards her.

Ravenna smirked, as though complimented. "You should have listened to her."

Lifting his hand, in a gleam of copper energy, Aaron conjured his own Athame. He raced at Isadora.

"And you can f– off." Using her power of Photokinesis, she sent him flying backwards into the wall. "Pilar." She called out to the Romani inside the protective circle with her two sisters, as well as Noah and Perry. "Bermuda, I need your–" Her words died when her power of Energy Manipulation sensed movement in the room.

"Put it this way, we've wanted to kill you for a very long time," Ravenna admitted, glaring at the young witch as she approached.

With a swing of her arm, Isadora sent the mature woman soaring backwards and watched her crash into the rubble of the broken wardrobe; the same one destroyed by Isadora earlier. Without warning, in the area between her and Ravenna, who rose from the floor, four demons manifested in ripples of energy as they teleported into the room.

"Kill her," Ravenna ordered in a shrieking voice. "Kill the witch."

Isadora's eyes widened with horror. Undertaking the demand, a male demon created a ball of fire in his open hand and threw it at the good witch. Gasping in fright, she activated her power of Transparency and Isadora became incorporeal as the fiery attack passed through her body, recoiled off the protective magic of the circle and shot back across the room. Struck by his wayward demonic power, the demon was vanquished in a shimmer of flames. Exhaling, Isadora's body became corporeal again and she quickly acknowledged the presence of her two children asleep in their bedroom. Would they be murdered too? She feared that if Ravenna had killed her cousin Shane and was now attempting to kill her, what would stop her from killing Isadora's two sons?

"Die witch," growled a demon.

Moving his arm back behind him, an Athame in his hand, he lowered to the floor, sliding his right leg out to the side. Whipping his arm out in front of him, he shot a dart of golden light at Isadora.

Raising her arms, and with a brisk flick of her hands, she used her Energy Manipulation to cause the dart to explode with a brilliant flash. It distracted the demons and she used her power of Transparency to turn herself completely invisible.

Noticing the witch's disappearance, the demons became cautious. Knowing she possessed the power to turn herself invisible, they weren't entirely secure with the idea she could attack without being seen.

"Pelasgus," Ravenna yelled as she hurried to Isadora's spot. "Find and kill the witch."

Released from Isadora's Energy Manipulation, Pelasgus let out a roar and used his vampire ability of Accelerated Movement to speed from the room. Hurrying down the staircase to the ground floor of the house, Isadora attempted to flee with her two sons.

A confused Owen queried, "Mama, where are we going?"

"We're going to buy some ice cream, bunny," she remarked nervously, fear evident in her voice as she continually glanced over her shoulder. "Quickly, first one to the front door gets two flavors." By the time she reached the bottom of the stairs, she noticed the front door was wide open. "Lyndon stop, honey." The fear in her voice was enough to make him stop and look at her. *Stay calm Indy, Get your children out alive*, she reminded herself. "Go! Go!" She urged her boys to hurry, running with them toward the front door.

Behind her, a fast moving blur flew down the stairs. Pelasgus grabbed her by the arm and yanked her back into his embrace. Owen was thrown to the floor as he lost the grip of his mother's hand. Isadora screamed in fright.

"Mama," a frantic Owen cried.

At the front door, Lyndon looked back and froze with fear as he observed the man with the horrible face holding his mother.

"Run! Owen, Lyndon, I need you to run," she ordered her children firmly.

Pelasgus smirked as he spoke in her ear, "Don't let them run away, I want them to watch me kill you before I kill them." He angled her head before licking her neck from shoulder to ear. "You taste like pineapple."

Mustering all the energy she could, Isadora let out a piercing scream, "Pridham."

He sank his teeth into her neck, feeding on her. "Pridham." She continued to scream.

"Let my mum go." Owen challenged Pelasgus. Revealing his magic, objects in the hallway began to elevate into the air, including the vampire. "Don't make me hurt you."

A demon exited the lounge room to the right, "Oh look, Pelasgus. The boy wants to protect–" startling the young child, Owen's Gravity Manipulation power spontaneously catapulted the man back into the lounge room. Slamming into the wall he cried out in agony as his body burnt up in a shimmer of flames.

A terrified Lyndon remained by the front door.

The elevated objects and Pelasgus suddenly dropped back down to the floor. Discarding Isadora's body to the floor, the cruel vampire smirked, blood drenched his lips. Accelerating forwards in a blur he slammed into an invisible wall of energy. Halted, he looked down at Owen in a pit of confusion.

"Powerful little–" began with a curious tone of voice. But then he suddenly cried out in terror and quickly shielded his face with his arms. "NO!!!" he screamed. A bold ray of sunlight shone in through the open front doorway, although it was night time.

Elegant and tall, Johdi Fox– cousin to Aaron, Noah and Perry from their father's side of the family– strode through the doorway with her arm extended out in front and her hand rigidly gestured. The slender witch was beautiful, had long brunette hair that fell in loose curls and an intimidating look in her youthful face.

"You will not harm a hair on that boy's head," she ordered, entered the house and stopped in-between Isadora's two sons. "Pridham, I have him contained," speaking she turned her head and looked over her shoulder as a young woman with long dark hair entered through the doorway.

Breaking free of her power of Fear Inducement, Pelasgus laughed manically as he named her. "Well if it isn't the beautiful nightmare, Johdi Fox! The witch who can turn a mortal man to stone and cripple you with your worst fears," They both exchanged a nasty glare. "Hello cousin!"

Moving Owen behind her, Johdi replied, "You're not my cousin, Perry is! You're just the vile other half of him!"

Pridham, the families Custodian stood in the background, closing the front door behind her. She silently observed with her amethyst colored eyes. Making a demonic growl, Pelasgus began to lunge at Johdi and with a brisk sway of her hand and aggravated facial expression she used her power of Petrifaction to turn him to stone.

"I said stay!" she yelled territorially and lowered her arm back to her side. "Now Pridham, take Isadora's children to the Romani Triad. I will secure the house." Pridham lingered in the back, silently, nervously listening. "Do you understand me?"

Pridham remarked uneasily, "Okay." Moving forwards, she placed a hand on each boy and magically vanished in a rush of white smoke.

Stepping past the stone statue of Pelasgus, Johdi raised her hand and pointed at him angrily, silently threatening to smash him into pieces. Lowering her arm, she turned her head and acknowledged the thick, black scorch mark on the wall. Closing her eyes, she used her other power of Magic Sensing to see how Owen had vanquished a demon. Opening her eyes, they glittered with blue and then she turned her head upwards as she sensed another good, magical individual upstairs in the attic.

"Pilar...!"

As an Omega Witch, Johdi's power proved potent enough to pierce through and observe those inside the protective circle. Retiring the power, her eyes returned to normal as she knelt down to close the eyes of a deceased Isadora Pogue who lay at her feet.

Upstairs, using the power of the Hellmouth to enhance her own, Pilar rose from her kneeling position on the floor; looking back she acknowledged herself with a certain stare. She was able to operate on multiple levels of existence. The first being an anchor on this plane while in a deep meditative trance, the second was an Astral Projection in Limbo and as consciousness that was able to communicate with the occupants of the room.

Standing toward the edge of the circle she observed the other individuals with a cautious, yet superficial look. "Something is not right," she communicated with herself, Noah and Perry in Limbo, "there are several demons here in Aaron's attic. There is a dead–"

In Limbo, Noah looked up at Pilar with a confused look as she stood over him. "Who is it? Are you able to identify the innocent?"

Pilar looked vague as she stared at nothing, "I think it is Shane." Looking across the room in the human world she was able to identify Shane by his face as his lifeless eyes stared back at her. *Gutted by the revelations as he cradled a deceased Bermuda, Noah cried out as his heart broke a little more.* Pilar continued, "I need to bring you back Noah!

"I'd rather be here then go back to nothing!" he growled nastily.

Pilar looked down at him and then ahead of her as the three remaining demons approached the circle while Ravenna stood back with evil written beautifully on her face. The demons held out their hands, conjured shimmering balls of fire and then unleashed their attacks at the protective combined magic of the circle. On impact with the invisible magical barrier, the fireballs made it flash white and ripple in individual places.

"Come to me, feel my power, I call to you, aid me in this darken hour," Pilar began to cast a summoning spell.

Answering the magical call of their sister's spell; Siobhan, Zane and Juliann suddenly manifested as Astral Projections inside the circle with their eyes filled with the blue energy of the Hellmouth. Scattered about, they all glared in the same direction as Pilar and focused their potent group power of Telepathy upon the demons. Unexpectedly their bodies twisted and they shrieked cries of pain while clawing at their heads. They met their end in shimmering flames.

"So," Ravenna strode forwards, stopping at the scorch marks of her vanquished demons, "you're the esteemed," her acid words complimented her perfect smile, "Romani Triad that I keep hearing about. It's an honor." Her attempt at an intimidating glare was oppressed by Pilar who now stood alone in the circle. The other Astral Projected Triad members had returned to their bodies.

Pilar spoke with repulsion, "Believe me, the feeling is not mutual. You're all class–" she hesitated as she acknowledged Aaron walk across the room and stand beside his wife. "Aaron, you cannot trust her. She is e–" again she fell silent as he shape-shifted into a woman with long black hair. "Who?- Now I understand!"

"I am Rasima Straig," Ravenna's sister introduced herself.

Pilar went to speak but fell silent as Rasima let out a scream and was suddenly turned to stone. Struck in the back, the stone figure broke into pieces and Johdi Fox appeared in the room. Distraught, Ravenna turned and swung her arm. Quick to protect herself, Johdi made contact first, punching the evil woman in the abdomen and sent her flying backwards with telekinetic force.

Returning to Aaron's house, Pridham, the Pogue Family's Custodian, this time was accompanied by Vesta, the Old One otherwise known as Aryan. Pilar turned her head slightly and winced, forced to use her telepathy to create a mental block because of the immense power that Aryan gave off.

"They're all dead," she revealed in a sad voice, "Melpomene killed them!"

Johdi and Pridham stood silent but their true, distraught emotions were displayed in their teary eyes and pressed lips. Aryan sighed with remorse and with a snap of her fingers...

~*~

P ilar looked down at the family's open Book of Shadows that lay on the floor to her side. The title of the page read: *'To Restore One from Darkness'* Holding her arms out in the air in front of her, she elevated her head with her eyes closed toward the ceiling as she took in the surrounding magic.

Time had been rewound!

"Place one of your hands on Noah and Perry," she instructed the twin witches. "Then, with the other, hold one another's hand. This will keep your power connected and also connected to the same dimension that both of these men are trapped in."

Bermuda and Andromeda nodded their heads and interlocked their free hands with one another. Revealing its potency, a magical force manifested with the sister's connection. So powerful that it tried to force their hands apart and for a moment gave off a magnificent golden glow. Pilar lowered her head; her eyes sprang open with a fierce strength captured within them and abruptly her hands latched onto Andromeda and Bermuda's forearms. The mild but forceful power she was channeling was nothing compared to the full force of the Hellmouth.

"Here now the prayer of light, may it call to you in still of night." The sister's cast the *To Restore One from Darkness* spell. "Victims who have fallen into blight, we restore you back to the world of light!"

Changing the course of the future, Aryan, invisible, reappeared and stood behind Aaron as he fiddled with a pink crystal that would leave Perry in Limbo but revive and unleash Pelasgus, his vampire side. With a gesture of her hand she caused it to dissolve into a glittering pink dust in his hand. Inside the circle,

Perry and Noah gasped as they awoke and sat up. Acknowledging the significant modification in time and what was supposed to happen; Ravenna, feeling threatened, took Aaron by the arm and fled, teleporting them both out of the house.

~*~

*I*n *Limbo, up in the highest point the churches steeple,*

Melpomene stood tall and full of grandeur as she looked down upon the colonial town square. Her eyes were full of despise and her long teal hair flapped about in the breeze.

"Welcome," she greeted the male dressed in a business suit, "Asmodeus, to my inspired dimension." He stopped at her side, free from his icy prison when his lover Paimon was vanquished. "What news do you bring from The Duodecim?"

Asmodeus remained quiet as he observed his surroundings.

FIRST INCARNATION

*O*n the floor of her house, Alera lay. Her coven members looking on in disbelief, confused as to why their affluent and powerful leader was suddenly dead. Teleporting into the residence, Rafaela, half-demon, half-witch daughter of the deceased leaned down. Removing her overhanging hood, long gazelle horns protruded from her forehead and her long brunette hairstyle; unusual for a woman of this time. The congregation stood in silent awe as they observed the evil power that they worshipped and revered as a demigoddess.

"What happened?" Rafaela queried in a hostile tone,

A woman replied, "We are uncertain. She sent Asmodeus to kill the Scarlet Witch, and then suddenly collapsed."

Her hostility increased, "YOU LIE. She has bloodied wounds. Which of you attacked her?" Moving her arm and opening her hand she created a shimmering ball of fire. "You dared to revolt against your own leader. After all she has given you."

The group became uneasy. They were innocent.

"But we did nothing," one exclaimed fearfully, "have mercy."

Screaming in frustration, Rafaela threw her fiery attack at the group. Outcries of agony filled the home and the followers were vanquished. Their black scorch marks stained the floor. Reappearing in another pulse of rippling energy, Rafaela manifested in her gothic, stone chambers in the Mesopotamian city *of Babylon*. In the Pogue Book and Romani of Shadows, it stipulates that this city was one of the original great cities of witches and also built upon a mystical Hellmouth. *She laid her mother upon the stone altar and her minions, the four cloaked Judges and three evil witches moved in to tend to the slain.*

"We're going to resurrect her." Rafaela revealed her motives, cleverly hiding her bereaved state. "The dark witch shall rise."

Over in the corner of the square room, a woman emerged from the shadows.

"My liege," she summoned, wearing rags for clothes. "This was her fate, Rafaela. You should not test the deities who have woven this destiny for her. There will be colossal repercussions."

Rafaela glared at her Oracle, "I do not care for your foresight, Oracle. My mother will rise again." Standing at her mother's head, she began to move her hands about as she closed her eyes, summoning the power of the Hellmouth beneath the city. "Bind to me and commit to my will, I summon you." She began her spell.

Removing her hood, powerful witch, Callidora spoke, "You've been gone for a while–"

"Where have you been?" interrupted Kailash, Callidora's sister. "Fleeing to the future to warn the witches won't save you."

The third sister Cissy simply glared at the foreseeing woman. In her brisk escape to the future; Kasi, the Oracle with the shining aura, had seen the future lives the three Penthal Witches would occupy but under the names of Connemara, Carmen and Kathryn.

Kasi pleaded, "My Liege," Rafaela ignored her for a few seconds, "I beg of you, leave the witch dead. I have seen your future, they will come, there will be four of them... from the future." Letting out a scream of pain, her body burnt up in a glimmering flame.

"This Babylon belongs to me." She reopened her eyes, revealing their full black nature as she received the power of the corrupted Hellmouth. "Let those good folk bring their armies and war, for I am the Demigoddess of the promise people. And I promise evil will rise beyond the confines it already occupies."

Across the desert, atop the tallest building in Jerusalem; the Romani Triad stood poised for war. Esmeralda D'hôte and her three sisters, Judea, Inara and Nera were the ancestors that the powerful Amedea Bonifacio, from which they would descend. Standing hand-in-hand, a magical wind blew their long hair about as they siphoned off power from the Hellmouth beneath Babylon to enhance their own potent telepathic magic. Their eyes were filled with brilliant blue energy.

"Nefertum, Atum, Ra." Together, they summoned Egyptian deities associated with the sun. "We call upon you in this sacred hour, lend to us, your power. Fuel our solar star." An unearthly groan quickly echoed throughout the Middle East. Beyond the confines of earth, out in space, a colossal solar flare was released from the sun and then magically reappeared within the focal diamond center of the talisman around Esmeralda's neck.

Allying with the Romani and stationing herself in Egypt, powerful sorceress Uphara – maid and protector of the future incomparable queen Cleopatra VII – drew on the power of the moon. And as Kasi predicted the four individuals from the future came to aid the witch of Egypt.

~*~

In the present day, Rafaela ambled around the perpetual white dimension of the Meat Locker, eagerly waiting for her mother Alera to cross the Limbo Dimension and appear in the Phantom Mirror where she could finally be released back into the modern world.

"Babylon was 'the' mantel of power," she put emphasis on, the, in her speech to Kamenwati. "Now it's this pathetic place mortals call, Treadwell. The hanging gardens of Babylon are something to behold. Truly breathtaking." Although pure evil, she administered a few words of regret. "I should have listened to that backstabbing bitch, Kasi. Don't underestimate Romani or Pogue Witches."

"They're mortal at their core," Kamenwati said with an evil smirk. "They have a weak spot, you just need to find and exploit it."

Rafaela paused as she glared at her minion for interrupting her. "If you were a witch or magic born, you were a descendant of a Babylonian. True power came from that city. None of this Pogue crap coming out of Egypt, bullshit. I can hear your thoughts, so please shut up. I should have known that...that... wretched Scarlet Witch was the daughter of Uphara."

"Your power is infinite," Kamenwati flirted with her leader. "Nothing can hold a candle to your greatness. Not even those Pogue Witches. I wish I had been present in your first reign of power. However, now, I am here to serve you."

Rafaela approached, grabbed the beautiful demon by the back of her head and kissed her passionately. One would assume a sign of appreciation for her servitude.

"Loyal servitude is rewarded with power my mother always said," showing no longing in her face, Rafaela pulled away and began to pace while Kamenwati longed for more intimacy. "My mother, Alera was the greatest witch in the Babylonian time. My father was a demon. I had no need for a reputation back in my day. I had my Dark Promise and that alone was enough to create fear amongst good. Today the only legend of my existence is in that thing people call Revelations—"

Kamenwati acknowledged, "You're the Whore of Babylon?"

"I was the first whore. A temptress some might say," Rafaela retorted territorially. "With the added power of the Penthal Sisters–" she looked at the Nightmare Soldier, reading her thoughts. "They will never find out if you keep your mouth shut. Gosh," the demigoddess sighed, as she pondered with a curious look in her face, "Connemara must be over a thousand years old by now... yet doesn't look a day over thirty. Slut," she chuckled, admiring her old friend. "A true and powerful witch is unique in their appearance."

Kamenwati remarked in a cloud of confusion, "Elaborate?"

"Indigo colored eyes," Rafaela revealed, "A Babylon Witch is distinctively powerful compared to any other level of witch. My mother and Uphara's daughter were Babylon Witches."

~*~

*I*n the ancient time, Rafaela, and her fellow Dark Promise Coven members Callidora, Kailash and Cissy held hands as they stood around the body of Alera. Together, repeatedly, they cast their summoning spell to harness the power of the Hellmouth beneath Babylon.

"From the skies the power came," their united voice was so enchanting, "down to earth for none to reign. Beneath the ground where power dwell, we call upon the mouth of Hell."

An otherworldly groan of something colossal resonated throughout the Middle East as the ground began to shake. The good witches of Babylon fought against the evil foes in the streets; but as Rafaela's evil outweighed the good, those opposed to the rising darkness fell to their death.

Across the desert, south-west of Babylon, the Great Pyramids of Giza were gigantic and wondrous in the moonlight. In her magical temple, hidden from mortals, Uphara, powerful sorceress stood at her altar waving her hand over a shallow gold basin filled with water.

"I call upon the power of those afar, show me Pluto, Venus, Saturn and Mars–" with a brisk flick of her hand she used her power of Molecular Combustion to create an explosion in the water. Outside, the clear night sky four individual stars became bold, brighter than the others as the respective planets lent their power to Uphara. "Through time and space," mentally wielding her power of Telekinesis, Uphara made the basin elevate into the air. "I seek their place," the basin moved away from the altar, "where Pluto lives at steady pace." With her mind she halted the basin and then threw the liquid into the air. "Where Venus lives for lovers chase, Mars is unkind, and Saturn is obscured in space."

Splashing against the fabric of time and space, the liquid created a portal into the future where three men and a woman stood in an attic with their backs to the Egyptian Witch, unaware of her presence.

A firm and curious voice spoke, "What do you think you are doing?"

"Transpor–"

Before she could use her magic to transport her future descendants through time and into the ancient world, Uphara was startled by a presence in her temple. Turning around, the portal to the future dissolved behind her as she was greeted by a woman, Atropos, a deity of fate.

"Grandmother," Uphara acknowledged cautiously with half an excited smirk. Atropos stood with her arms folded. "What-what brings you to my temple?"

Atropos was tall, slender, dressed in a short, white Grecian dress with a hemline way above the knee and golden armor shoulder plates. Her long golden blonde hair was placed in a messy ponytail with a crown of golden laurel leaves.

"Uphara," Atropos began in a blunt tone, "you are well over two-hundred years old and incredibly ignorant. It was your intentions, which I sensed, that brought me here. I watch and see everything. I am fate. Do not make me annul your power like I did your mother's. But your daughters on the other hand are fraying my last nerve."

Uphara gave her grandmother, Atropos, one of the four original witches – otherwise known as the Venefica –a sour stare. The beautiful blonde woman before her could easily, at the snap of her finger, remove her existence from the world.

"I was going to summon our future descendants," Uphara revealed her intention. "We could use their power to aid Esmeralda and her Romani. With the combined power of the Solar and Lunar Star Talismans we can destroy the Hellmouth beneath Babylon. Releasing it from Rafaela's influence, vanquish–" she choked on her own words as she thought about what she would say next.

Atropos raised an eye brow, "You would vanquish Lindsay and Alera, along with Rafaela to prevent an inevitable apocalypse?"

Uphara roared, "We need the power." Then as she took a step forward Atropos moved her hand in a swaying motion as she used her power of Energy Manipulation on her granddaughter, making her abruptly stop in her tracks. "You used magic on me."

"Be quiet," Atropos growled.

Elevating her face to the ceiling, she closed her eyes and silently summoned.

Uphara said in a meek voice, "The gods of witchcraft will not like you using power."

Lowering her face, a magical wind blew around Atropos. Opening her eyes, they shone with golden energy.

"I am the power. I rule over the Gods of Witchcraft. I am fate," she said in a deep voice. "Across the skies, of black and grace," she began to cast a spell, "I call upon the planets and summon you to this sacred space." Extending her arms up, she then brought them down as she executed her incredible power. "Bless us with your presence, Saturn, Pluto, Mars and Venus."

Outside in the night, in the skies over Egypt there were four brilliant flashes of light. A fiery purple glow raced down, swerving in its descent, it swooped around and the colossal power crashed into the sand. A tall and masculine man stood with a fiery purple aura, purple energy burning his eyes and the symbol of Pluto glowing on his forehead. He wore plates of armor on his shoulders with leather straps that crisscrossed over his chest and around his back. He had a leather strap around his left forearm down to his wrist while his attire below was a leather Roman skirt and knee-high boots.

The resemblance to Noah Pogue was incredibly precise. After all this was his first incarnation as the planetary deity Pluto.

A second, third and fourth fiery light, one golden, one red and one green raced down from the sky and crashed into the sand.

Tall individuals, two males and a female stood with fiery, glowing auras and glowing eyes dressed in similar attire to Pluto. But the others had the symbols of Saturn, Venus and Mars on their foreheads. Respectfully, Venus was Perry's first incarnation and Mars being Aaron's. But the unknown blonde haired female figure as Saturn was yet to present herself in the future timeline.

Powerful and commanding, Pluto stood in front.

Magically they were teleported away in a pulse of energy as Atropos brought them to her in Uphara's temple. Reappearing moments later, the small assembly of planet deities stood opposite Uphara. Deactivating her immense power, the gold energy left Atropos' eyes and the magical wind ceased.

"Impressive," Uphara murmured with a smirk.

Atropos gave her granddaughter a sour stare as she turned her head to acknowledge the new arrivals. Standing face on to them, she gave a stern look of power, making it obvious she was a person of significance and should not be crossed.

"I am Pluto," he said pompous and powerful, "God-king of the galaxy."

Atropos shot him down, "And I am Atropos. Deity of Fate, I am capable of erasing you from existence." He softened his hard stare while the others behind him immediately felt intimidated. "You're aware of–"

Venus interrupted, "I could smell the stench of the evil here on earth from my throne but to be here, it's enough to decay the flesh from your bones." Turning his head as he looked about, he halted his sight on Uphara. "How do you survive with it?"

BATTLE FOR BABYLON

Some time prior... Rafaela and her congregation of evil witches - in their temple beneath Babylon - had magically acquired the deceased body of Lindsay Hogue and laid it beside Alera's. Their hands were placed over one another and bound together with a red piece of fabric to create a tether.

"Two together, now as one, with the power of the Hellmouth, thy will be done." They cast a spell.

~*~

*T*he dirt covered ways of Babylon were strewn with bodies of good and evil witches. In the distance there were cries of pain and explosions as the battle escalated in other lanes of the city. Leaping down from above, an agile young woman with long brunette hair landed on her feet in a cloud of dirt and observed her surroundings. Behind her a burst of black smoke manifested and a male demon appeared. Remaining still, she glanced out of the corner of her eye and pretended not to sense his presence.

He lunged at her as he cried out.

Turning around quickly, she swiftly extended her arm with a gestured hand. He was struck by a pulse of energy and posed rigidly as the power of Eloquence slowed his molecules down to the point that it looked like he was frozen in time. With a snap of her finger she used her second power of Molecular Combustion and caused his body to explode into a fireball, vanquishing him.

"The Hellmouth belongs to free folk of Babylon," she yelled.

In her first life, Kalena was a powerful witch, in the future, her second life, she would be rewarded the powers of a Custodian, go by the name Pridham and continue to protect innocent people.

Leaning slightly to the side, she evaded a fiery attack.

"Babylon belongs to Rafaela," said a territorial man. "From here evil shall thrive."

Twisting her body slightly to the left, she then twisted back to the right, using her power of Levitation to spiral up into the air, narrowly missing the blade of a sword wielding demon. She hovered for a moment, observing the Neanderthal below her. Behind him, a second version of her appeared. Stabbing him in the back with her Athame, she vanquished him in a fiery display. Before her clone could return to her body, a sudden explosion blew dirt into the air making Kalena shriek and covered her eyes as the dirt stung her face. Letting out a groan she was pulled downward unexpectedly. When the dirt settled, she lay on the ground, at the feet of a monstrous Minotaur.

The beast began to lean down toward Kalena. Overhead, something flew across the sky with brilliant wings and roared like a lion. A small explosion of light against the Minotaur's chest caused it to stagger backwards and let out a roar. Looking up and ahead it acknowledged a gallant cougar with large eagle wings. Reaching up onto its back legs, its body glowed and it magically assumed the figure of a beautiful woman with long blonde hair. The Custodians had come to Babylon to even out the war and rescue the fallen.

She spoke, "I am Renae Ketch." The beast laughed at her. It could crush her in an instant with its brute strength. Her figure was slight while its body was large and bulging with powerful muscle. "I will beat you Minotaur."

Renae swayed her right arm slightly back behind her and then swiftly brought it around as she extended it out in front, aiming her open hand at the beast. Activating her powers, she fired a Light Dart - a technique achieved with the power of Photokinesis - striking the beast in the chest again, this time the force of the attack flipped it over. Crashing into the ground a cloud of dirt blew upward. Teleporting out of sight in a rush of white smoke, Renae reappeared beside Kalena; kneeling down, both then disappeared in another rush of white. Levitating back up onto its feet, the Minotaur let out a roar that caused energy surrounding it to ripple violently.

"Oi, ugly," a female voice came from above. "Up here. I am Grace Leighton. Princess of the Dragons. A free folk of Babylon."

Turning around and then looking up, the beast snorted loudly as it acknowledged a woman with long auburn colored hair and gladiator armor. Using her magic, the woman's aura burned a fiery red and she shape-shifted into a full size, adult dragon; a creature known to the magical community as a Beastial. A Celestial Beast. Its large clawed feet gripped the roof of the building causing the walls to splinter under the heavy weight. Opening up its massive wings, it extended its long neck and growled as its large eyes eclipsed the Minotaur. With its mouth open the dragon breathed a torrent of ferocious flames down onto the beast, obliterating it instantly.

~*~

Through the streets of Babylon a woman walked, her hair so long, thick and styled in loose curls. Her eyes full of black. Each stride was elegant as her gown of black dragged in the dirt around her feet.

"Oh to tempt, it gives me pleasure," she sang to herself as she walked along, "to seduce a man with lace and leather..."Tthe foundations of Babylon shuttered beneath her feet as her *unyielding evil grew to maximum potential. With a sway of her arm, she used her dark magic on a good witch. Hit by a pulse of telekinetic energy, the innocent woman's body became rigid and twisted; her bones breaking and killed instantly. "Being good won't protect you from the weather."*

Atop the buildings, Princess Grace Leighton of the Dragons - in her full colossal beast form - let out a bellowing roar and breathed flamed down at the vile woman that walked beneath her. With a brisk sway and gesture of her hand, the woman, extinguished the flames and used her power of Telekinesis to throw the massive celestial creature backwards from the roof and into the desert beyond.

The massive dark object moved through the moonlit night. Her impact with the ground caused a slight tremor and sent an impressive explosion of sand into the air. The only thing that alluded to the presence of the large object in the sand was its massive wings that had become spread out as it lay still. In the area surrounding the magical creature, vigorous flickering flames rose up from the ground as more Dragons in humanoid forms came to the aid of one of their fallen princesses.

"Come to me, on bended knee and worship thee," the woman halted in the center of Babylon. "For the Hellmouth beneath, is bound to be me." A few lingering good witches staggered about the fallen. A witch with the power of Electrokinesis threw bolts of lightning from his fingertips at Alera, only to have her body absorb it. "Let me tell you a tale, of a lady so fair from a town so bare. From the First World her powerful ancestors came," with a brisk hand gesture she caused the innocent male witch to explode into a fiery display, "But Atropos was weak compared to what I am capable of," she announced arrogantly.

A second witch turned and attempted to flee the city. Magically, Alera manifested ahead of him while he had his head turned, looking back over his shoulder.

"Why try to out run your fate?" she queried, he collided into her and was jolted back by a pulse of telekinetic energy. "You know you will ultimately die, right?"

He gazed into her captivating black-filled eyes, void of anything remotely human. Suddenly, he began to gargle and blood spilled over the corner of his lips. Moving her arm back toward her, she had disemboweled him at his point of impact with her and with a brisk sway of her hand she snapped his neck. With a satisfied smirk, she watched him drop dead onto the ground.

"I was born a Stealth Witch, something greater than that of you diminutive lower breeds of witch." She spoke aloud as though addressing a nation, but only deceased bodies lay before her. "I am 'The' beast. I am," her voice deepened with power, "the Hellmouth. And I will devour this world."

A large supercell storm began to blanket the sky over Babylon. Thunder rumbled and lightning flashed. Behind Alera, a mysterious mass of snow and ice manifested quietly as another surviving good witch approached. Sensing the magic, she turned and acknowledged the desolate center of the ancient city. Bloody, dead bodies littered the ground. Turning back around a woman with long white hair and piercing blue sapphire eyes stood before her.

"I am Säde. The Ice Witch of Babylon," the woman announced in a curt voice. "And hell just froze over."

Briskly reaching her arms out in front she unleashed her magic on the evil witch. From her open hands icy energy streamed imposing force and the cyrokinetic witch turned Alera into a sculpture of solid ice. Lowering her arms to her side, she appeared pleased with her efforts. The harmonic whistling of birds drew her attention upwards as Custodians soared over, eagerly waiting for the witch's cue for them to land to heal the wounded and nearly dead.

To the side of the ice manipulating witch, an abundance of red, sparkling astral energy quickly manifested as the Scarlet Witch, Lindsay Hogue, appeared. Her long blood red hair levitated in a spiritual wind. Her fixed stare was intimidating.

"STOP!" Lindsay yelled, extending her arm and gesturing her hand. "You need to leave Babylon."

Säde replied, "What do you mean? This is our city." Her eyes full of despise, "Who are you?"

"I mean, this witch and her evil surpasses more than any of us have known." She turned her head and looked at the ice sculpture. "I am Lindsay Hogue, sister and adversary to this here fiend. Her daughter, Rafaela, the Whore of Babylon has used dark magic to bind us to the one body."

Säde growled, "You're with her?" Readying her hands to use her magic on the redhaired witch. "You helped bring about the destruction of our sanctuary. Our city."

Lindsay sighed and looked remorseful, "I tried to protect it. But you cannot fight this evil. It's not your responsibility. It is their duty. The two tribes destined to protect the Hellmouth. The Romani and my mother, Uphara. With the power of the Solar Star and Lunar Star they can destroy the Hellmouth beneath Babylon."

"I have enough power," the woman growled nastily.

Lindsay replied, this time just as rude, "Are you stupid girl? She has bound herself to the Hellmouth. What you see, is literally her, as its physical form on this plane. Alera can and will wipe you clean from existence as long as she controls what is beneath you. There is no good here, just evil."

Making harmonic whistling calls above in the night, outside of Babylon, in view of the massive archway entry into the city, the nine, celestial, winged cougars swooped down and as they touched down onto the desert sand took on the form of beautiful men and women. The men had blue sapphire eyes, the females had amethyst colored eyes and wore white flannelette robes.

Sensing their approach, Säde turned toward them and raised her arm; gestured her hand, signaling them as she called out, "Stop. Don't enter the city."

Swiftly swinging her arms out with gestured hands, she used her powers of Cyrokinesis. Her eyes shone a brilliant wintery blue and her long white blonde hair blew about as a magical dome of ice encased Babylon. Within the city snow quickly fell, turning the hot desert citadel into a winter wonderland. Those evil battling good were turned to solid ice from the falling snow.

~*~

A woman, slender and tall with caramel blonde hair, somewhere within the city battled a heavily cloaked demon. She spun around on the spot, revealing a piece of material covering her eyes. Upon her swift rotation she grunted as she forcefully kicked the demon. Extending her right arm upward, in a gleam of white energy, the long silver blade of a sword emerged. Swinging her body around she went to strike the concealed figure with her weapon as falling snow quickly blanketed the ground.

"Remove the rag," the creature growled in a deep voice, grabbing the blade of her sword. "I want you to see me, the demon that will take your-" Its words were cut short when a snowflake, upon landing on its head, instantaneously turned the demon to solid ice.

With a grunt she pulled her sword free, shattering the demons hand into red, bloody pieces of ice. The young woman stood for a moment as she observed the foe before her.

"I am a warrior. I'd sooner die with a wound to my back than stare into the eyes of an individual who I let get the better of me." And with brisk one swing she shattered the demon with her sword, vanquishing him. Pulling her blindfold up to her hairline her indigo colored eyes were revealed; this acknowledged that she was one of the rare few dubbed Babylon Witches. Turning her head and looking in one particular direction, she magically sensed the Ice Witch named Säde. The multi-storey mud brick buildings were dusted with snow and outlined by superficial moonlight.

Behind the young woman, dressed up like a beautiful Egyptian goddess, the Old One Maria manifested in an abundance of white light, *"My child, you must leave."*

"This is our home." The woman looked out the corner of her eye. *"It was that mongrel Rafaela who brought evil here. Took our city from us. They must be driven out and back into the Underworld."*

"The time of Babylon has come to its end. The Hellmouth beneath the city will be destroyed. But your destiny continues." And with those words, Maria transported the young woman out of the citadel.

~*~

Within her icy prison, Alera's eyes began to glow red and her invisible aura revealed itself by the rippling atmosphere surrounding her as it began to heat up and melt the ice. Letting out a sudden gasp, Lindsay leant forwards slightly and held her hand to her head as an agonizing pain streaked through her mind.

"Ugh!" she groaned, revealed through her power of premonition, *"The Romani are attacking."* Seeing them atop a

building in her mind with a brilliant golden light surrounding them. "You need to leave or you will die."

"I will not leave Babylon," Säde, powerful and intimidating with her fierce glowing eyes spoke in a blunt and unyielding voice.

Lindsay pleaded again, "She will slaughter you without a second thought."

Säde remarked nastily, "This is our kingdom. It does not belong to evil."

Letting out a scream of agony as pain surged through Lindsay's body and magically her body exploded into glittering red astral energy that quickly moved and absorbed back into Alera's frozen body. Elevating up from the ground, the Ice Witch of Babylon called upon a Babylonian Deity to increase her power.

"Goddess Antu." Her seductive voice was fuelled by power. A malevolent wind picked up suddenly and howled like a banshee. Thunder exploded behind the blanketing storm clouds and multiple bolts of lightning struck the town. "Lend to me your power, hear me in this sacred hour."

On the ground below, surrounding Alera's frozen body, the air rippled as she expressed a heat from within to reduce her icy prison that dissolved into wisps of evaporating steam. Reaching her arm up, with a disgruntled look upon her face, Alera gestured her hand into a clenched first at the Ice Witch. Suddenly, letting out a scream, she was ripped down from the air and forcibly slammed into the snow covered ground at Alera's feet.

Extinguishing her power she stared up at her foe.

"Clever, little, witch," Alera oppressed her opponent with a bigoted glare. "Did Maria teach you that trick?" She smirked sarcastically and curiously. "Turn the Hellmouth to solid ice so its power is nullified."

Deep beneath the citadel of Babylon, in the gothic crypt, as Rafaela, Callidora, Kailash and Cissy continued to perform their *spell to siphon the power of the Hellmouth the icy effect from Säde's power crept up the walls, across the ceiling and over the floor. Feeling her feet turn to ice, Cissy shrieked and disconnected herself from the spell. The connection to the colossal energy beneath them was severed and as a result the four women were thrown backwards.*

BATTLE FOR BABYLON – PART TWO

Together, hand in hand, Esmeralda D'hôte and her three sisters, Judea, Inara and, Nera stood atop a mud-brick building with brilliant golden auras that glimmered like sunlight in the dark of night.

"Nefertum," Esmeralda chanted.

Judea summoned, "Atum,"

"Ra," Nera's voice had a seductive echo.

With her arms out in front of her in a welcome gesture, Inara commanded, "In this hour," a colossal and otherworldly groan moved about the Middle East as their incredible power reached its peak, "the earth shall know who has the ultimate power."

Together, in perfect synchronization, their glowing auras ignited into ferocious and dancing golden flames. Their eyes enveloped with glowing sunlight.

Below, in the streets of Jerusalem, shadows darted about, Lazarus- King of the Vampires in the area and his group, under the instruction of Rafaela, were closing in to kill Esmeralda and her sisters, eliminating the threat that they posed to unleashing hell on earth. Darting from one shadow to another, a female vampire, clad in rags, slid in the dirt as she stopped, growled hungrily and looked up at the four women atop the building the next street over from her.

"From the ground," Inara sensed the presence of the vampires, "raise a wall, made invisible and to scald." Her glowing eyes fixated on the snow dusted Babylon in the distance.

Sprinting out of the shadows in a blur with her vampire ability, Accelerated Movement, the female vampire slammed against an invisible barrier. Scalded, she screamed out in agony as she disintegrated into burning pieces of ash that floated away in the breeze. Accelerating down the wide, dirt road, the devilishly good looking Lazarus in his warrior armor, leather and bare, developed chest, stopped with a dark glare upon his face. Multiple shadows sped out into the moonlight and abruptly stopped as the group of vampires stood with their king.

"Kill the others," Lazarus spoke in his knee-weakening deep voice. "But leave Esmeralda for me. I want her for myself."

~*~

*O*verhead, in the night sky, a shooting star manifested and then quickly disappeared. Soaring down from the heavens, Spectra, Goddess of the Stars levitated in the air, camouflaged by the black canvas adorned with little, twinkling stars. She had been the very star that moved across the sky as it entered the earth's atmosphere. Her long and thick auburn colored hair hung over her right shoulder with a crown made up of stars that twinkled in her hair. You could have sworn they were diamonds. Expressing her attitude through her eyes, their indigo color deepened to a sensual purple and her nude colored lips were crumpled with dissatisfaction as she observed the silver outlined figures below.

"I can feel your power." Turning her head and attention away from the vampire activity below her. "Who are you?" The air and black canvas of sky behind her rippled as an Egyptian inspired chamber quickly took form around her. "I name you deity, Atropos, of Fate." Her feet touched the ground and the warm, illuminating light of the sprawling room shone against her warrior attire of leather, white gold metal shoulder and breast plates, skirt of chiffon-like material, roman sandals up to her knees and metal wrist guards. "What right," she retorted, levitating, she accelerated across the way toward Atropos with a sudden look of arrogance, "do you have?" Wielding her immense power, the deity gestured her hand at Spectra and stopped her abruptly.

Atropos glared at the young deity. "Stars are such fickle things. They're either a long and enduring burn or quick." Both females continued their threatening looks. "Which are you, Spectra?"

Uphara interrupted, "ENOUGH!" irritably. "This is exactly what Rafaela wants, us to turn on one another."

"Fine," Atropos remarked sarcastically, as she released her hold over the auburn hair deity, "you can live a while longer. I've already sown your fate, girly."

Deities, Pluto, Venus, Mars and Saturn stood at the stone banister of the open balcony with their back to the three women behind them, as they quietly with stern expressions observed the snow dusted Babylon. Pluto, hearing the heightened conversation behind him, turned his head to the side; his deep, blue sapphire eyes pierced Spectra's mind.

"Daughter," he addressed her formally. "It would be wise not to tempt fate."

Uphara, standing by her altar looked ahead at him with a curious expression while daughter Spectra turned her head and gave a cold stare. Moving around the stone table, the Egyptian witch moved across her lair and stopped at another object before addressing those who were present.

"Everything is in place." Although a mere grey octagonal shaped top, positioned on a waist height marble column, the sundial before Uphara was about to become a symbol of immense power. "If we're going to do this, we need to do it now."

The planetary deities turned their back to the war on the horizon and placed their attention on the witch clad in a white ceremonial gown and golden, Egyptian inspired, jewel-encrusted tiara. Atropos and Spectra stood back as they observed. Uphara gestured her hand as she summoned the deities over to her so that they could fuse the artifact and compass points with their individual and godly powers.

"Mars, guards the north," Uphara spoke as she had swayed her hand at the N symbol engraved in the surface of the sundial. "Do you bestow the stubborn power of Deflection?" she queried him.

He nodded his head once. "I d.," And he placed his hand willingly upon the symbol.

Uphara then looked at Plut., "Pluto, guards the south." Swaying her hand at the S symbol engraved in the surface. "Do you bestow the instinctive power of Probability?"

Approaching the sundial in the middle of the room, Pluto stopped at its side, opposite to Mars and then placed his hand upon his designated symbol. "I do."

Venus approached, stopped, and held his hand over the symbol marked, E, for east.

Uphara spoke, "Venus, guards the east. Do you bestow the lurid power of Sensazione?"

Venus replied, "I do." He placed his hand down on the engraving.

At the banister of the balcony that overlooked Egypt, gorgeous goddess Saturn stood poised with her long blonde hair cascading down her back. Her Roman warrior attire both hugged and accentuated her slender figure. Silently sensing fate summoning her, Saturn, with a longing stare, took a deep breath, nodded her head and then turned away from the world below her. Her thoughts were fuelled by the goal of being triumphant against the forces of evil that Rafaela commandeered. There was confidence in each step that she took toward the Sundial in the middle of the room. Her eyes swam with ego and power. Stopping in front of the engraved symbol of W, she looked ahead at her brothers.

"I, Saturn, Bestow the strong-willed power of Tangibility."

Uphara standing between Pluto and Mars - her eyes full of white glowing power – arm quickly extended out in front of her and gestured her hand rigidly. Her long hair blew about in a fierce magical wind.

"Align together; be as one, we call to you, sacred moon." Uphara cast her spell.

With all their hands now placed down on their allocated symbols, a brilliant, moonlight glow shone out of the magical device and enveloped the entire room. The moon was full and high in the sky over Egypt. Blasting through the tip of the pyramid, the energy and light of the Sundial was absorbed into the moon. Inside the temple, Uphara stood at the powerful magic object, her eyes still full of power, hair blowing about and arm still extended forwards. The four deities had sacrificed their lives; their bestowed powers had fully charged and weaponised the witch's artifact.

"GIVE IT TO ME!" she yelled, ordering the moon.

Two of Uphara's many powers were Photokinesis and Gravity Manipulation, mentally and physically she had control over the moon and the light it emitted. Over her right shoulder Atropos stood side on, powerful and full of pride with her arms folded and posture stiff. Her long blonde hair blew about. An unearthly groan moved about the arid landscape as a colossal beam of magical energy surged out of the moon and into the pyramid below. Passing through the ceiling and with monstrous force, the moonlight energy slammed into the Sundial where it was absorbed.

~*~

*O*ver in Jerusalem, sensing the activation of Uphara's powerful magic as they stood atop the mud-brick building, the Romani Triad: Esmeralda and her sisters, surrounded by flame-fused energy of the sun began to levitate into the air. Shoulder to shoulder, hand-in-hand, they were united in their power and fierce with their presence in the young town.

"Cometh the hour, unleash thy power," the voices of the four gypsies echoed loudly in their unison. "Will of the sun, four burn as one."

There came a magical swirling noise as the flaming energy surrounding them gave off a glow and gathered in the center of the talismans. A colossal groan followed with a deafening explosion, a potent pulse of energy was expelled from the sisters and a beam of glittering, copper colored energy shot out and surged in the direction of Babylon. Sprinting around the buildings with their ability of Accelerated Movement, several of Lazarus' vampires cried out in pain as the pulse of energy given off by the Romani struck them, causing their bodies to explode into molecules that scattered in the wind.

An angered Lazarus skidded to a stop in the dirt after using his own Accelerated Movement. Being more powerful than his young kin, he was able to avoid any injury from the energy-based attack.

"Esmeralda." His calm human facial features stressed as he assumed his horrific vampire visage. "Count every single breath, because your last one will be mine."

Deep beneath the citadel of Babylon, in the gothic crypt lit with moody candlelight, the three sister witches Callidora, Kailash and Cissy groaned as they pulled themselves up from the floor after being thrown from their magical connection to the Hellmouth. With ease and unaffected, Rafaela swiftly levitated back up onto her feet with a hostile glare and her eyes full of black. Reaching her arms out in front she caused the air to ripple violently with her powerful black magic as she resumed her connection to the Hellmouth without the aid of the witches beside her which she had previously required.

"She used us." Cissy was outraged.

Suddenly powerless, Kailash brushed her hair from her face, "You stole our power."

Standing in-between her two sisters, Callidora realized the error of her evil ways. Before she addressed Rafaela, she caught a glimpse of ghostly apparition of the deity Pluto in his gladiator attire. By the look of regret in her face it was revealed they'd loved one another once before she chose evil over good. Quickl,y he vanished. Sensing the witches behind her, Rafaela, with her mind caused the three of them to scream out in pain and buckle back down to the ground. Kailash and Cissy combusted in flames and were vanquished. On the floor, screaming in pain, the blood red, Amour Talisman - gift from Pluto - around Callidora's neck shone and protected her from the evil of Rafaela. Rising back up, she stood poised against evil, renewed as good.

"Beneath me, hear me, as above, so below, I sway and power flow." Elevating her forearms and gesturing her hands, Callidora revealed that she too could wield significant power. Overhead and below, surrounding Rafaela on the floor, a ring edged in white appeared. Callidora continued her spell, "From this world I cast away, evil spirit." The white ring on the ceiling and the one on the floor suddenly shone.

Forged by Callidora, Sanction Circles - white circles edged into the ceiling and floor with a Babylon Crystal, directly over one-another, while channeling divine power could create portals and bridges to other dimensions in order to travel or banish entities.

Feeling the active magic, Rafaela's body suddenly contorted. "What are you doing to me, you wicked bitch?"

Callidora smirked confidently. "Removing your purchase on this dimension you demonic harlot." She briskly flicked her hands as she provided more power to her spell. "No longer may you stay, banished from this world, another dimension shall keep you at bay."

Letting out a scream as her arms flailed at her sides and her back arched, Rafaela was swallowed by a ripple of energy, banished to another dimension along with her four Judges. The glowing circles went dull as the divine power being channeled was relinquished. Succumbing to the affects of Säde's ice power, Callidora's body was quickly overcome by ice and then shattered, killing her instantly. The walls began to groan and then crack as the structural integrity of the building became compromised. Moments later the ceiling gave way and the gothic crypt collapsed in on itself.

The beautiful white haired, Ice Manipulating witch, Säde, looked up at Alera with despising eyes. Elevating her hand to her mouth she went to blow icy particles up into her foes face, but letting out a sudden scream she was magically dispersed into icy molecules that scattered about a wind. Alera appeared intrigued and confused by the sudden happenings. Behind her, on the horizon and completely unaware, the glowing, magical beam of powerful moonlight of Uphara charged across the desert toward Babylon. In the opposite direction, a glowing beam of magical sunlight surged with the city its target.

"Bound by two, tether she," a male's voice, deep and imposing moved behind Alera as it cast a spell upon her, "I tear in two, the pair of you–"

Swiftly turning around on the spot, Alera extended her arm. "Watch your tongue." Her powerful black and evil magic growled and cracked like a whip but was nothing compared to the potency of her opponent. "You're unaffected by me, how is this?" She kept her arm firm and hand gestured.

The man dressed like the Prince of Persia finished his spell, "AND SEPARATE THEE!" yelling as he abruptly spun his gestured hand.

Spontaneously, Alera's head rose, she arched her back and her arms became rigid as she was overcome with immense pain. Red energy shone in her eyes and her aura burned just as brilliantly. Pulling away at the right, a grey blurred figure manifested and flashed with light. Now separated back into two individual forms, a beautiful red haired Lindsay Hogue stood beside her twin sister.

"I am free..." she sighed with a smile of relief.

Alera's eyes filled with black and a hostile expression rose in her face. Her conquering of Babylon was at an end, but at a cost, now the full force of the moon and sun were about to destroy the city of magic and the Hellmouth beneath it.

"Who do you think you are?" Alera's sarcastic voice deepened with power, "The Prince of Saudi Arabia? No one has the power to separate us."

He spoke, "I am Rathe." His posture was proud and his muscles bulged with power. "I have more than enough power, I am an Old One."

Alera stood with her hands on her hips and a displeased stare upon her face. Her eyes were full of eternal black. Swiftly reaching her arm forward, she gestured her hand as she revealed a pink Babylon Crystal that both levitated in the air and spun around. A sudden magical wind blew her hair back and her facial expression became more sinister and oppressive. Extending her other arm out to her side she gestured her hand at Lindsay Hogue. Drawing on the power of the crystal Alera caused it to give off a glow and the red-haired witch beside her to scream out in pain.

"The witch and the Hellmouth are—" Alera's words were cut short as a beautiful and blinding glow engulfed the citadel and all its surroundings. Surging across the desert at both sides of the city *and Hellmouth beneath it, the power of the Sun and Moon made full and colossal impact with the city.*

In a devastating explosion of light and energy, Babylon was obliterated along with anyone who lingered within it. A blinding light shot up into the starry night sky, the Hellmouth was expelled from the Earth and sent back up to the heavens. The ancient and magical time of Babylon was now at an end.

~*~

Some centuries later...

A *mass of light which many could have been convinced of was a comet, plummeted down from the sunny, clear blue sky over a sprawling, parcel of land hemmed in by mountains and golden sandy beaches. Absorbed into the earth on impact, the mystical Hellmouth that was once beneath Babylon was embedded back into the earth. This rural paradise would become known as Treadwell and all things magical, good and evil would come to claim its significant power.*

On the sandy shore, a magical abundance of red astral energy manifested, a handsome and tall man clad in colonial American attire took form. Nathaniel Eames, prominent ancestor of the Pogue Line of Witches, had felt the call of the Hellmouth, he and his descendants would become its new guardians. Stepping out of the forest that adorned the foothills of the mountains, another, handsome gentleman, a Romani - clad in colonial attire and a maroon bowler hat on his shaggy mop of hair - had felt the call too.

FEAR NO NIGHTMARE

Treadwell in the month of March was still relatively warm as it descended toward wintery months, tonight it was a sticky sixty-nine degrees. The ground was still a little wet from the intermittent showers of rain that happened throughout the day with a top of ninety-five. Twinkling stars and a full moon adorned the night sky as a soothing, gentle breeze moved about the city streets.

Levu, a highly popular, retro inspired, nightclub that only played music from the seventies, eighties and the nineties in the city's East End was putting out an alluring vibe. Outside, the building appeared square in structure but on the inside, it was circular. Patrons entered through a revolving door and once inside were faced with a vast ceiling of hanging vines and branches decorated with clear fairy-lights and fancy disco balls. Around the nightclub were lounges and cushioned boxes that people sat on. In the middle was a big circular stage that shone a myriad of colors. The modern white bar with an illuminated countertop was at the rear of the establishment that curved with the wall.

On stage, a group of magical women dressed in seductive attire and fantastic hairstyles, the Siren Sorority, performed their rendition of Bananarama's 1986 hit song 'Venus'. Wind blowing up from the surface of the stage had their clothes and hair floating in a mesmerizing exploit.

Mortals danced around the stage with a hint of red energy in their eyes.

Through the doorway, the Nightmare Soldier, Kamenwati, dressed in an alluring brown leather skirt and a grey colored vest that asserted her breasts. Her hair was done up in a sleek and modern bun. She carried herself rather egotistically and her eyes looked down on people like they were cattle for her to harvest. Kamenwati gazed about the dancing mortals before her, looking for a victim. Something drew her attention quicker than she expected because she formed a smile and then ventured deeper into the nightclub. To the right of where the beautiful Nightmare Soldier Demon had stood was a cluster of square cushioned bar stalls. There, a suspicious leggy woman with caramel blonde hair sat with her legs crossed, her white sequin dress glimmering under the lights; she had observed the evil entity while sipping on a glass of champagne.

Through the crowd, Kamenwati slithered like a snake toward a male in the back of the club. Her pristine eyes were full of self-assurance much like a sense of superiority in the way she carried herself while walking. Just a few steps ahead was a man she'd sniffed out from the moment she walked in the door. From behind he had a styled mop of dark brown hair, a groovy eighties shirt and black leather pants. Kamenwati smiled spontaneously as she approached, extending her arm she went to tap him on the shoulder but then, suddenly stopped dead in her tracks. The smile replaced with a look of dread.

In her white sequin dress, the woman who had been sipping her glass of champagne slipped through the crowd behind the Nightmare Soldier, her presence giving Kamenwati a supernatural chill. It came across as a warning that there was a force of good close by. Glancing out the corner of her eye, the beautiful demon captured a silhouette of white before it disappeared in amongst the dancing mortals. Moving her attention back onto her desired victim, Kamenwati was disappointed as she acknowledged he had departed.

~ * ~

Elsewhere, in another dimension...

"**Y**ou're an absurd," Rafaela's voice snapped at Kamenwati's ear, "little demon-child. I've never known anyone to stare idiotically into the void of nothingness, like you do." The horned she-demon, dressed in a beautiful black gown observed the Nightmare Soldier opposite her.

Blinking her eyes, Kamenwati returned from where-ever-it-was that she had ventured off to mentally. Confused, before she replied to her superior, she turned her head and glanced about the familiar sights of the Meat Locker dimension she and Rafaela had been occupying since Eisheth's departure at the hands of Ryder Romani.

"I-I," she stuttered, bringing her attention back to Rafaela. "Forgive me, my liege. I was adrift. Away with the fairies, so to speak." She seemed somewhat confused and then showed a sign of repulsion. "Vile, bloody creatures." Looking up she was taken back as she witnessed Rafaela shape-shift into another woman with brunette hair, slight figure and about five-foot eight tall. "Who the—"

"If I do say so myself... " And with a brisk swing of her arm she used telekinesis to launch the Nightmare Soldier backward. "You definitely do not live up to your wicked reputation, Kamenwati." Johdi Fox, powerful witch, niece of Gregory Fox and cousin to Aaron, Noah and Perry Pogue is a formidable woman known to take down the strongest of tyrants with her ability of Fear Inducement. "You know what, I deemed you more powerful than this. I've had you under my spell for three weeks now—"

Swiftly rising back up onto her feet, Kamenwati retaliated, "Get out of my head, WITCH."

With one brisk hand gesture after another, she fired powerful bolts of black lightning. Johdi smirked confidently as the electrical power charged toward her. Glittering blue energy rose in her eyes as she used her power of Fear Inducement on Kamenwati. In a flash, the two woman switched positions, and struck by her own power, Kamenwati let out a scream as her body absorbed the full supernatural charge before exploding into a mass of black smoke.

~*~

Screaming in agony, Kamenwati, tied to a chair, was catapulted through the air and crashed into an invisible barrier and then crashed back onto the floor, breaking the chair she was bound too. Lifting her head and flicking her hair back, the Nightmare Soldier assumed her intimidating form, black eyes, gaunt facial structure, pale skin and dirty, shredded rags. Levitating back up onto her feet, she hovered from the floor and letting out a piercing scream,

"Do you seriously think," she snarled, lingering in the air, ghastly and ethereal, "a Spirit Prison is going to contain me, you stupid bitch?" Racing forward, the glow given off by the ring of white candles, a Spirit Prison, burnt her hands, screaming again, she hovered backward. "What is this magic?"

Outside the circle the dimension of white, the Meat Locker washed away and a dilapidated warehouse presented itself. Narrowing her eyes as she hovered back down to the ground, Kamenwati observed a shadow that walked toward her from afar. At first it was just a heavy black silhouette without any description, but the closer it got, the figure wore a baggy, hooded cloak and a set of long gazelle horns on the individual's head.

Resuming her mortal appearance, Kamenwati became nervous and slowly took a few steps backward, fear tightened her throat. Although powerful and self-assured, the Nightmare Soldier had just then inadvertently given away one of her very few fears to the witch who had imprisoned her.

"Rafaela... " she whispered, eyes wide and her face a shade worse than white.

~*~

Three weeks prior...

*A*fter Bermuda and Andromeda performed the 'To Restore One from Darkness' spell and bringing Perry and Noah back from Limbo, there was an uneasy atmosphere in the house, evil was closer than the brothers had first thought. But who and how, let it get that close?

Upstairs in the attic, Johdi Fox stood at a table cluttered with vast potion ingredients and a bubbling cauldron over by the window. Isadora Pogue stood at another table a little further away holding her hands over the map of Treadwell. She used her power of Photokinesis to cast a light, hoping that photons would grab at a location and reveal Kamenwati. To Johdi's left, intermittently, she would observe the Book of Shadows and mutter the scripture to herself as she reached about the table adding things to her brew.

"I'm going to find you," she grumbled to herself, "and I'm going to make you pay for what you have done." Reaching across the table, she took a pinch of dandelion.

Unsuccessful, Isadora closed her hands, deactivating her power. "I got nothing, again. Usually when I scry with my Photokinesis a demon or evil entity appears as a little light bulb on the map. Kamenwati is very good at cloaking her presence or is not in this dimension." Turning away from the smaller table, Isadora approached the opposite side of the table her second cousin was working at as she spoke, "Will a locator spell be strong enough?"

Johdi moved irritably and spoke, "Oh, don't worry, Isadora. I have a motive to find her. So my spell will work." Both of them exchange a certain stare. Kamenwati had burnt the Pogue Family. "Into shadows, dreams and hells," Johdi began her spell, "behind the veil, across the divide, into another world, is where she resides. I call upon the powers that be, find for me, Kamenwati." With her final ingredient and completion of the spell, the brew created a powerful bang and flash of light.

Gasping, Isadora was thrown backward across the room and crashed into the cupboard, demolishing it. Johdi turned away to shield her eyes from the light. Extending her arm she fanned the smoke away and once it cleared, she gasped aloud as she acknowledged the woman suddenly standing in the room.

"Who are you?" she queried cautiously, her hand elevated and finger pointed. Time was still, Isadora and the collapsing cupboard were still. Johdi's gentle nature suddenly became territorial. "Whatever you want, you won't get it here."

A soft smile formed on the unknown woman's face. She had a gentle aura around her. Not intimidating, the woman just stood there, silent and observing the witch.

"I am," and then she spoke with a voice that washed the room in peac,. "I am Deific."

Johdi didn't know what the hell a Deific was and wasn't about to show a welcoming demeanor. For all she knew this woman could be a demon pretending to be a divine being.

"And what the hell is a Deific?" Johdi growled. "I cannot say I know what one is, let alone recall ever meeting one, before... " She waved her hand about nervously at the woman, "...you."

The woman spoke again, "Treadwell is built on Hellmouth." Johdi narrowed her eyes, she knew this already. "I am," the woman again, this time slowly stepping forward, "one of just a few totems, invisible to mortals and magical folk that are spread about the area."

"Is this going to be," Johdi became sarcastic, "a long history lesson? Because I was, kind of, actually, trying to find a demon." She gestured her hand at the woman. "Then you showed up..."

The woman spoke, "Johdi Fox. A beautiful witch, gifted with the power of Fear Inducement. You've brought many tyrants to their knees. One thing you should have been given was patience," the witch narrowed her eyes nastily, "shall I continue?" The woman was suddenly shown obedience as she crossed the room, stopping opposite Johdi at the table. "The Leviathan, or Hellmouth, is pure magical energy, easily swayed to either side when provoked as proven by Alera. You do know that Treadwell is Babylon reborn?"

Johdi interrupted, "Are you friend or foe? Because how do I know you're not some rogue, power hungry deity looking to bring about an Apocalypse?"

"First there was the powerful three," the woman continued, "and then came The Old Ones. When they lost their purchase on this reality thanks to the evil Potentate, the occupation of the Deities came about. But between the Old Ones leaving and the rise of the divine beings, we, Deific, nurtured the earth back to a place of beauty and serenity. We've come and gone throughout the ages. We sleep and we wake. We walk multiple dimensions at once. There are many... many, levels to the magical echelon that you ought to be accustomed to." Johdi gestured her facial features, impressed by the story the woman told her. "But let me warn you, there are many evils closer to you than that of which you are aware."

Johdi replied curiously, "You're the Grand Design...?"

"Vanquishing Kamenwati, will only remove today's threat. Tomorrow's threat still lingers in the mirror," said the woman, missing the witch's question. "I will help you, but it will not be without consequence."

Johdi expressed subtle impatience, "Do you know where to find Kamenwati?"

"You just did." The woman smiled, telepathically placing a thought in Johdi's mind before vanishing in a swift flash of white light and time resumed itself. With a heavy thud, Isadora demolished the cupboard and then fell onto the floor.

Looking to her side, Johdi observed the mirror on the wall.

~*~

Trapped inside the Spirit Prison in the abandoned warehouse, Kamenwati placed her hands at each side of her head as she used her demonic black lightning power to override her mind to obliterate her fear of her superior, Rafaela. She could feel the witch, Johdi Fox altering her mind and senses.

"Set thee free, let thee soar, in the shadows, nightmares call," Kamenwati reached arms out rigidly as she cast her spell, drawing power from the shadows, "let the dark blow out the light."

Heeding her call, shadowy figures began to emerge from the gloomy walls that escaped the poor light that shone in through the broken and dirty windows of the warehouse. Quickly, moving in on the Spirit Prison, the lanky things set about blanketing the dancing flames atop the candles and extinguishing them. Watching the shadows dissolve into the ground, Kamenwati smirked as she approached the edge of the circle made up of half melted candles. She extended her left leg over and placed her foot down on the other side. Stepping out fully, she felt a sudden sense of freedom.

"Stupid witch," she mocked with an arrogant tone. "I find your Fear Inducement most dismal–" letting out a scream, she was struck in the side by a bolt of light and catapulted into a spin before crashing onto the ground. "Ugh!" she groaned, stricken with pain.

A confident Isadora stood proud with her arms folded, "You occupy a corporeal form on this plane, which means you're not immune to the powers of a witch." Sarcastically she taunted the demon, "Don't tell me you forgot that?"

Looking up at her opponent, battered and bruised, Kamenwati winced, wounded from the witch's photokinetic power. Light can inflict great pain upon darkness. Feeling intimidated and out-matched, the Nightmare Soldier attempted to flee. Her eyes shone red and abruptly her body turned into a ghostly, black mist. Kamenwati tried to flee into the shadows only to be struck by a pulse of energy and painfully forced to resume her mortal figure. Screaming aloud in agony, she crashed onto the ground. Confidently striding out from behind one of the many concrete supports that held up the warehouse, Johdi lowered her arm and hand as she approached the demon.

"How is this going to end, Kamenwati?" Johdi's voice was smug although so sensual. "You decide. After all, it's your swan song."

Kamenwati looked up at her foe with a dirty face splattered with blood.

Isadora spoke as she approached from behind, "You deserve to know what kind of pain you have brought upon our family."

Swiftly, resuming her black, ghostly mist form, Kamenwati just as abruptly returned to her mortal body in a standing pose while struggling to stand her ground. "Your attempts to cripple me with my fears will only go so far."

Johdi asserted, "I haven't even finished yet," and she shape-shifted into Rafaela. Swiftly extending her right arm out in front with her hand rigidly gestured, she exercised her power of Fear Inducement. Levitating up from the ground, her body contorted with pain, Kamenwati screamed out in agony. Her aura shone a brilliant crimson colour. "I don't fear nightmares, nightmares fear me."

~*~

*I*n a flash of light, Kamenwati entered a new illusion created by

Johdi's power of Fear Inducement... With her eyes shut, she felt herself twirled about by another as disco music played amongst the void of black. It began with the sound of thunder, rain and lightning. The sound affects faded and then the song awoke with a great disco beat as the Nightmare Soldier opened her eyes.

On stage in Levu, Isadora twirled and danced about with a microphone in her hand singing Amii Stewart's song, 'Knock on Wood'. Her long auburn hair and indigo colored eyes seemed to glow under the myriad of disco lights. She wore black suede knee high boots and a white dress with tassels sewn all over it so that when she moved, they all fanned about. Showing off her power of Photokinesis, glittering photons circled her as she played with them in her free hand.

Behaving like a mortal, oblivious to the reality she was in, Kamenwati danced about the dance floor with a male who was yet to show her his face.

FEAR NO NIGHTMARE – PART TWO

*O*n the stage in Levu, Isadora paraded about, dancing and twirling in between male and female back up dancers. The men were dressed in tank-tops and jeans, while the women were clad in a bra and skin-tight, satin leggings. Fans inside the stage blew air upwards, hugging them with a mesmerizing wind.

Amongst the crowded dance floor, Kamenwati danced with her male companion. He took her by the hand and pulled her in toward him, twirling her as he went. With her back to his chest they swayed their hips. He kissed her neck. Twirling her outwards, he released her to the dance floor. Dancing and turning around on the spot, she caught a glimpse of her suitor. Abruptly stopping, she stared at him as he stood amongst the dancing patrons, staring back at her with a wicked grin. He was Perry Pogue.

"You've got to be," she puffed with slight exhaustion from dancing, brushing hair from her face, "bloody kidding me. If you're objective is to torture me with, Perry Pogue, then you're a bigger idiot than I thought you were, JOHDI FOX." She observed him cautiously. Suddenly, his facial features morphed into his vampire visage.

Johdi's voice licked up the right side of Kamenwati's neck, "I know your fears, and being rendered mortal is one of them." The demon stiffened uneasily.

Johdi mocked, "Because it means your powerless."

Making an hungry growl, Perry, in his vampire visage, accelerated toward the Nightmare Soldier. Throwing her arms forward, Kamenwati tried to throw her bolts of black lightning to propel him away. Powerless, she screamed as he grabbed her by the arms, pulled them out to the sides and sunk his teeth into her neck, feeding on her blood. She screamed.

~*~

I n the real world, in the attic of Noah Pogue's home, Kamenwati sat slumped in a chair in a Spirit Prison; her head hung to the side as a bloody mark appeared on her neck. In an instant the bite wept and blood dribbled down to her shoulder.

Isadora stood with her arms loosely folded. Her long auburn colored hair pulled back into a ponytail; she wore a white button-up, long sleeve shirt and skinny, dark denim jeans. Tapping her foot implied her lack of patience. Beside her, Johdi stood with her eyes consumed with red energy as she projected herself into Kamenwati's mind and manipulated her fears.

Elsewhere... In the picturesque suburb of Summit Hills, thirty minutes east of Treadwell city, a real estate sign had sat out the front of Aaron Pogue's house for three weeks stating that it was now up for sale. Under the cloak of night, as the crescent moon lay on its back foretelling rain high in the sky, a sedan pulled up with its bright headlights lighting up the street. The engine ceased, the lights went out, the door opened and closed as a woman exited. Long burgundy hair fell in fuzzy curls down both sides of her face, the rest pulled at the back of her head in a bun. Her pretty blue eyes glittered in the moonlight. Estia Bradmore, a unique specimen, was a clairvoyant-medium and new owner of the ex-Pogue house whose origin came from Adelaide, Australia. She was wearing a summer dress with a short hem-line; a moss green knitted shawl over the top and mushroom colored, suede ankle boots with a six-inch heel.

"Estia...." a gentle voice whispered on the wind, "Help them...."

Looking ahead as she stopped at the start of the driveway, Estia acknowledged the ghostly aura that glimmered at the two storey house's outline. A creaking noise broke the silent night and her eyes drifted toward the front doors. She observed them curiously as they suddenly opened, as if by magic, on their own. Walking the length of the driveway she swayed her arm out, creatively gestured her hand and a crystal ball appeared in a magical glow as she approached the entry.

"Beyond this world that we cannot see," Estia began to cast her spell upon the house, "I use the ball to gaze, send a beacon through the haze, come to me spirits, and speak with me."

The crystal glimmered with a pretty greyish-blue energy and like a beacon- it pulsated, casting out the energy. She observed it wash against the walls, floors and ceilings and then return back to the ball in her hand.

She closed her eyes. "Come," and stepped into the house, crossing the threshold the lights magically came on inside the house, "into the light."

Reopening her eyes, she had crossed the magical veil that separated the human world from the Spirit world. She suddenly found herself standing on the footpath of Patricia Street in a wintery downtown Jasper, Alberta, Canada in the day time. In magical wisps of spirit smoke, Bermuda Pogue appeared behind her left shoulder, Andromeda behind her right.

"Help...." Bermuda whispered in Estia's ear.

Andromeda murmured, "Us...."

Aaron suddenly stood in front of her. "Please."

Gasping, Estia opened her eyes again, standing in the doorway of the house she had purchased. Ahead of her, the same ghostly visions of the twin sister witches appeared for a moment before disappearing.

~*~

Inner city Treadwell had become increasingly busy since the Solstice Gala had crossed paths with the assembly of V8 racing cars that came to town to challenge the annual Treadwell Master Cup (TMC). Sitting at an outside table at the trendy, Durango Bar on Loden Street, Perry and Noah enjoyed a cold beverage after their seemingly never ending nightmare of being trapped in limbo. Perry sat there, admiring certain women that caught his attention as they walked by and inadvertently revealing his secret bisexuality to his brother, he also gazed upon some single men that walked past every so often.

"Perry," Noah queried, taking a swig from his long neck bottle of beer, "I have a question."

Turning his attention back, Perry stared at his brother, curious to see what would be asked. He leant forward, took his bottle of beer, had a sip and then placed it back down before sitting back in his chair again.

"Shoot," he smirked, "what is your question?"

Noah, for a moment, looked over his brother's complexion with a curious look on his own. "I love you regardless of whom or what you are. Vampire or witch." Perry gave him an odd look, wondering where this question would go. "Tonight, I've been observing the way you look at women and then I noticed the way you look at men too. Now I know you love women, and I know you love sex with women. Probably multiple at once-"

Perry turned his head slightly. "If you're asking if I am a man whore, then you've probably answered your own question without evening having to ask it."

"Are you gay?" Noah blurted out, then with a second thought, "No hard feelings if you are. I'm just asking an open question."

Smirking, Perry paused for a moment and then replied, "I like men and women. I am probably," he drank some more from his bottle of beer, "bisexual if I am completely honest. I've had boyfriends, sure. I've had girlfriends too. For me it's about energy, sometimes you cannot control what attracts you. It just happens. Sex with both genders has been a satisfying adventure for me." Noah sat with an interested expression on his mature face, it was a surprise but inside he felt totally at ease. "Wow. That was easier to say than I thought. I've always kept myself closed away from... you, Aaron... family, etc. I feared the nightmare of being ridiculed. It's what Aaron has done to me my entire life."

Noah formed a frown, "You feared how I would treat you?" He had a look of hurt, "Perry." suddenly as they both exchanged a look, and Noah couldn't have expressed a better look of being proud and accepting of his brother than flashing a smile. "You are my brother. I have loved you since the moment I held you in the hospital when you were born. I couldn't care less if you were gay." Perry smiled, feeling butterflies in his stomach as he felt flattered by his brother's response. He felt empowered. "Come, let's go."

Rising from their chairs, both brothers finished the last of their beers and departed Durango, heading toward the eastern parklands.

Entering through the iron gates of the Treadwell Botanical Gardens, the two brothers took a casual stroll along the tree lined, bitumen path that was well lit by intermittent garden lanterns. They talked about life and unimportant things in the world. They laughed on occasion. Suddenly, a woman's scream further on into the garden stole their attention, they stopped in their tracks as silence pursued.

"Do you sense anything?" Perry looked at his brother.

Noah looked about for a moment as he focused his Custodian powers and then turned his head to look at his brother. "Do–" Before he could finish, Perry snatched his hand and utilized their united power to enhance both their ability to sense magical and mortal entities. Both their eyes glittered with magic. Suddenly Noah spoke, "There." He pointed ahead but toward the right side of the path.

~*~

Screaming, the three beautiful Wood Nymphs being attacked by a small group of male demons evaded flying balls of shimmering fire. Out in the open, in the large clearing of the botanical gardens, the demons and magical creatures played a deadly game of Russian roulette with the exposure of the supernatural to the mortal inhabitants of Treadwell.

A male demon held out his hand. In a gleam of copper colored energy, he conjured an Athame. Gripping the hilt of his weapon, he threw it at the red-haired Wood Nymph. Letting out a scream of agony, impaled in the chest, she was vanquished as her body was ravished with shimmering flames.

"NO!" cried the blonde Nymph. With a brisk swing of her arm in retaliation, she unleashed glittering golden energy of Nature Manipulation upon her opponent. "Go to hell."

Abruptly, a swirl of green energy manifested between the Nymph and the demon. With her hand raised and bold glare upon her face, Madelyn Romani grabbed the glittering golden energy and dispersed it as she manipulated it with her own magic.

"Flee," she commanded the remaining Nymphs. They disappeared in gleams of green light. Turning, as she lowered her hand back to her side, Madelyn glared at the demon. "You idiots never learn do you?" Swiftly elevating her hand again, spinning it as she went, she commanded tree roots to burst up from the ground, surround the demon and rip him back down. He cried out in pain as a belch of flames flickered up from the closing hole in the ground.

Beside her, older sister Serene, Autumn Elf Queen manifested in a similar glow of green energy. Her long blonde hair was braided and decorated by a few leaves, and she wore a green dress adorned with brown lace and sandy colored ankle boots. Extending her right arm forward, she projected a stream of yellow, corrosive poison. Splattered with the liquid, the demon cried out as he clawed at his body as it began to steam. After a few agonizing minutes his body melted into the ground.

Turning around, Madelyn was struck in the arm by a fireball, screamed and crashed into the ground.

"In this place, on nature's mound," with a gesture of her hand at the straggling female demon, Serene completed her vanquishing spell, "slaughtered victims, pull thee down."

The female demon's aura shone with golden energy. Spontaneously, hands clawed out of the ground and grabbed the demon by the legs. Letting out a scream; she was pulled into the ground and vanquished in ravishing flames. Quickly kneeling down, Serene turned her sister over and observed the wound on her arm.

"Are you okay, Maddy?" she queried in a soothing and motherly voice. "I will call for Renae, she can heal you."

Madelyn lay on her side, wincing from the pain. "I'll live, it's not my first and definitely not the last war wound."

Looking up, Serene called out to the night sky, "RENAE. I NEED YOU."

Heavy footsteps pounded the ground behind the two sisters, running across the dewy lawn, Perry and Noah came to the aid of their friends. Irritated at his brother's mortal speed, Perry grumbled, grabbed his brother by the hand and hastily accelerated both of them forward with his vampire abilities. Stopping in an instant, a few seconds later, both brothers suddenly stood right behind Serene as she tended to her sister.

"What happened?" Perry queried, letting go of Noah's hand. "Are you okay? We heard a woman scream." Behind, Noah wobbled for a moment as he fought the nausea brought on by moving with accelerated speed.

Serene sat Madelyn up as she began to talk, "Pilar and the Triad have a demon named Slither, held captive. They're..." she hesitated awkwardly for a moment, "they're using creative measures to get information out of him to find the whereabouts of Brady. Tonight, his demons were here, killing Wood Nymphs."

Perry realized, "Because killing nature sprites would lure the Romani out in the open–"

"Leaving Slither unprotected so that Morgana could retrieve him," Serene implied. "But we intercepted the demons so that Pilar and the others would not have to leave their post. It is torturing Pilar, not being able to find her son. His location is cloaked even from the might of the powerful, telepathic, Romani Triad."

Serene and Perry exchanged a stricken stare of concern.

~*~

*S*creaming in agony, Kamenwati tried dismally to grip at Perry's hair as he fed on her blood in the nightmare reality that fear manipulating witch, Johdi had her trapped in. The patrons in Levu were the first to magically dissolve away in wisps of supernatural *smoke before the captivating, retro club of Levu swayed like water and became a tempered Canadian forest of towering Douglas fir, Western Hemlock and Western Red Cedar to name a few.*

Kamenwati summoned the strength and pulled Perry from her, throwing him away, his body spiraled and vanished into a magical mist that scattered in the forest. Feeling a little nausea from the constant transition of surroundings, Kamenwati staggered for a moment as she regained her clarity.

"I know your fears, Nightmare Soldier," Johdi's voice whispered against her ear, "Fear of Mortality, Fear of Vanquish, Fear of Greater Evils than yourself. You're a weak specimen, Kamenwati, a pathetic demon."

Listening to the voice, the regal Nightmare Soldier's eyes turned black, her face became gaunt and black crawled across the ground as it seeped out of her. Her attire morphed into torn, dirty rags and her long hair unraveled as it began to float about the air.

"Do you honestly think, for a wretched second, you bubonic bitch, that you have won? Overcome the Nightmare that is me, Kamenwati." Extending her arms, the Nightmare Soldier cast a pulse of energy from her body, into the forest.

Released in the real world, from the Nightmare Soldier inside the Spirit Prison, the pulse of energy struck Johdi and sent her backward across the room. Impervious to energy-based attacks, Isadora passed through it. With a painful groan, Johdi slammed into the wall and was rendered unconscious. Acting on instinct, Isadora vanished in a flash of photokinetic light and then reappeared inside the Spirit Prison with the demon.

Swiftly, she lowered her head down to Kamenwati's left ear and hissed, "Fear not the nightmare, but the bitch that is one. Because I'm sure as hell no daydream." Straightening her posture, she placed each of her hands at either side of the Nightmare Soldier's head. "I call to thee," suddenly she felt herself connect with power beyond the confines of the house and Isadora's pupils dilated, "powers that be, aid me." Her power of Photokinesis became active and her hands gave off a glow.

In a flash of light, Isadora manifested in the reality Johdi had trapped Kamenwati inside of. Swinging her right arm forward as she assumed an aggressive stance, her hand shone and she fired a slender dart of light at the demon.

Impaled in the abdomen, the black, evil that seeped out of the Nightmare Soldier hastily receded as she buckled from the immediate attack. She resumed her more human-looking form and observed the blood on her hand after she touched the wound.

"Being mortality wounded, really does suck, hey?" Isadora mocked her sarcastically. "Welcome to life as a human being. The very things you prey on for sustenance."

Kamenwati spread her legs a little to better balance herself as she felt herself become severely weakened by the torture Johdi had put upon her as well as Isadora's Photokinetic power.

"You have no idea what is coming, you poor thin." And for the first time Kamenwati appeared humanized in her tone of voice, showing sympathy toward Isadora. "I will tell you what I achieved, that way you can better understand why I was asked to do what I did."

Raising her arm and gesturing her hand at the sky, Isadora fired a bolt of light and commanded, "Release thee from thy binds, return thee to proper space and time."

Letting out a stricken gasp of air, Kamenwati awoke and Isadora's hands were slightly repelled from either side of the Nightmare Soldier's head, severing her connection. Quickly, she exited the circle and an unconscious Johdi came to and rose back to her feet.

"You've achieved," a battered, bruised, bloodied and wounded Kamenwati acknowledged the two witches as they returned to the Spirit Prison's edge, "what you wanted, you merciless cow. I smile at you Johdi Fox, you're far better than I originally gave you credit. You're definitely the epitome of Fear, I must say."

Isadora barked viciously, "Get to the point."

Johdi silently observed with mostly curiosity but there was caution in her eyes.

"Back," Kamenwati spoke truthfully. "Back all those months ago when I abducted Prometheus... or Perry as you'd call him, it was under the instruction that Rafaela wanted to unlock the nightmares he had the Sognare Coven in Los Angeles lock away."

Johdi replied, "I remember as a child, that his nightmares would render him catatonic from time to time. They were intense. Lindsay and Greg were fearful that they might have had to commit their son. He would mutter on about a woman named Alera who would come into his room. Whisper to him stories about an ancient city named Babylon. How he possessed a rare power called Sensazione. A curse placed upon the Pogue Family of witches that–"

Kamenwati continued, "Every witch who possessed the power would be reachable to her. That the power allowed the user full access to their brain, make them significantly more powerful than the common witch. Human beings only have access to one side of the brain, not both. Many ancestors before Aaron, Noah and Perry possessed the power, the majority of them succumbed to Alera's torments. She'd reach them from the other side."

Isadora questioned, "How?"

"Mirrors," Kamenwati replied, she coughed and struggled for a moment. "Every witch who possessed the power was born a twin. Usually the one that survived birth was the one tormented by the other who died at birth. Alera would use the twin-connection to seduce the living one into using the power for evil. They believed Alera was their twin trying to contact them. On the rare occasion, there was an ancestor who possessed the power and both twins survived."

"So being a twin balances out the power?" Isadora queried.

Johdi interrupted, "The power is a curse; it's supposed to drive the user insane. Not one person is supposed to possess that much mental power."

Isadora realized something. "Bermuda and Andromeda are twins."

"Bermuda is the possessor of the power, and Andromeda balances out the affect," Johdi revealed.

Kamenwati finished, "It was in his dreams that Alera showed him how to resurrect her and rejoin her and his mother, Lindsay. You see, the two witches were twins. In Ancient Babylon, in their first incarnation, they were rivals. Rafaela tethered them to the same body, believing they'd become the ultimate force of evil the world had ever known. And it worked for a short period until the Old One Rathe divided them. They destroyed Babylon, almost laid the entire good supernatural community to waste. But in separate bodies they are just Stealth Witches. That is why Rafaela had me do what I did."

Isadora spoke again; realizing Rafaela's intention, "Rafaela wants to resurrect Alera." But then the theory became vague for her. "But place her in Perry's body? ...Suddenly I'm lost."

"No," Kamenwati struggled as she coughed, slowly dying. "Perry also knows the location of where Lindsay is buried. Rafaela is Alera's daughter. She wants to bring her mother back along with Lindsay and have the two of them become the ultimate force of evil again. And if she achieves this, Alera...Lindsay, the both of them together in one body–"

Johdi replied, "Will corrupt the Hellmouth and bring about an apocalypse."

Kamenwati coughed and then spoke, "She has what she needed. But vanquishing me will not stop the threat of Alera's return. Like the Deific told you, there is still tomorrows threat that lingers in the mirror– ARGH!" She screamed out in sudden agony; her body succumbing to the wound and was ravished by flames as she was vanquished.

"If only Bermuda were here–" Isadora reminisced about how Bermuda would always catch Aaron standing in front of the mirror in the lounge room.

Johdi cut her off, a hint of remorse in her voice, "Well Bermuda and Andromeda are both dead."

In the Treadwell Botanical Gardens as Serene, Perry, Noah and Madelyn Romani lingered in the distance on the lawn; two heavily cloaked and ominous figures stood on the bitumen path watching them.

Behind Perry and Noah's back and unseen by Serene and her sister, a grey mist began to materialize as it spiraled up from the ground. Black buzzing molecules and fiery red flames quickly intertwined. Assuming its form, a man clad in a suit and salt and pepper hair straightened his tie and buttoned-up his suit jacket.

With a flick of his wrist, he threw Noah to the left with telekinesis and Perry to the right. Observing Serene's quick defense, he shoved his hands forward, throwing the two women backward onto the grass.

Perry made a hungry vampire growl and accelerated himself at the demon. Grabbing him by the throat, the humble gentleman smirked as the Pogue witch gargled.

"Do not test me, boy. I am Asmodeus." And he threw him like a ragdoll onto the ground. "Consult your precious Book of Shadows. Come find me when you're ready for a proper fight." And in a fork of lightning he was gone.

Chapter Eight

FACE OF EVIL

"Veniat ad me (Come to me)," Pilar Romani and her siblings chanted in Latin. "Hear my call. I summon power great and old, from this city that is home, only to borrow, not to own."

In downtown Treadwell, sitting at a table drinking coffee with some friends, Ryder Romani suddenly felt an explosion of power inside. She closed her eyes, trying to suppress the bizarre sensation. A feeling of a million volts of electricity coursing through her body and like her skin was on fire. Her mortal friends laughed and conversed about fashion, television shows, celebrities, health and fitness and men. Spontaneously opening her eyes, she vanished from her seat, teleported away with the aid of magic.

Letting out a shriek, Ryder reappeared in the Bocca dimension; a place of perpetual white and then a disembodied groan resonated as something colossal made its presence felt. Silence immediately followed.

"Oh you've got to be kidding me," she growled in protest, knowing that the Triad were unknowingly using her as a conduit to summon the power of the Hellmouth.

~*~

The octagonal shaped attic of the modern Romani plantation mansion was alight with soothing golden light. A strong sense of good was afoot. At the center of the room the hostage named Slither sat bound to a chair.

Some hours prior, downstairs in Pilar's kitchen, the four siblings conversed.

"He is a Superior Level Demon," Juliann stated the obvious without remorse as she sat upon the counter top.

Pilar, standing in-between the sink and the island in the middle of the kitchen spoke with a firm tone. "If he has hurt my son or—"

Siobhan, regal with her long blood-red hair flowing over her shoulder sat on a barstool. "Pilar," she snapped with narrowed eyes. "We all need to remember that he is our brother. He is two-faced. Sheppard has seduced us with false impressions. If we're going to remove the knife from our back, then we're going to have to do it properly."

Pilar growled nastily, "I want to false impression his face." Spontaneously her powers caused the glass vase on the sink to explode. "I am sure Morgana will come for him."

Juliann smirked, "She could always send your in-laws to harass you again."

Pilar shot her a vicious glare.

"We need to be careful how and what power we use against Sheppard," Siobhan, the voice of reason of the family made a valid point, "as well as Morgana. Summoning the power of the Hellmouth has been a deadly game of fate, as shown with the loss of Bermuda and Andromeda—" The comment made Pilar move uneasily, feeling responsible for teaching the twin witches to

harness the power of the Hellmouth to enhance their own twin-magic. "I say, we use our combined Telepathy. We don't attack or approach Morgana head on. We use Sheppard to our advantage."

Zane entered the room in a hurry, "Morgana is trying to lure us away from Slither." His sisters looked at him cautiously. "Her demons have surfaced in the Botanical Gardens."

Siobhan turned away from her brother and looked ahead at Pilar. "What could possibly be there—" gasping sharply, her power of Premonition became active as it forced her eyes shut.

Astral projecting herself into her vision, she saw the Treadwell Botanical Gardens at night. A group of Wood Nymphs were being attacked by an assembly of demons. Screaming, one of the nymphs was vanquished in ravishing flames.

Gasping sharply again, Siobhan was released from the vision.

"What did you see?" Pilar queried.

Siobhan replied, "Wood Nymphs." Her voice fuelled by confusion.

~*~

Back in the present...The four Romani stood shoulder to shoulder in the attic, hands interlocked and their eyes consumed with the blue mystical essence of the Hellmouth. With the aid of their innate ability of Omnilingualism - to speak and understand any language - they continued to cast their spell that would open up Slither's mind. Their Latin perfect to the T. Before them, their family's Book of Shadows sat on its stand.

"Open up his rigid mind," a magical wind suddenly blew about around them, "all the thoughts that intertwine. Reveal what secrets hide."

Bound to the chair, with his head hung, Slither began to laugh as the spell failed to take effect. Separating their hands, the four Romani parted as they walked around their book of witchcraft and began to take up the four compass points around their prisoner. Their eyes back to normal now.

"You possess no real power," he taunted, laughing at them. Swiftly he withdrew his hands from behind his back, rose from his chair and paused for a moment to admire his release. "Morgana has freed me." He looked ahead, exchanging a smile of gratitude with an invisible vision of the evil Morgana. "She protects my mind from your magic. You pose no threat to—"

Time suddenly stopped...

Morgana smirked egotistically as she approached Sheppard Romani. "Tsk. Tsk. Tsk." She clicked her tongue and waved her index finger. "You're an idiot, Slither." He gave her a glum look. She suddenly stopped her moving finger and aimed it toward the ceiling. "The Spirit Prison is above you." Sheppard moved his head and looked up at the circle of white candles and their dancing golden flames directly above him. "What can I say, I wear two-faces; I smile at you with one and then drive a knife in your back with the other."

From inside the Bocca Dimension, Ryder was able to observe the goings on in Pilar Romani's attic. Her relatives and time were frozen. But then her attention was swiftly drawn to Slither as he suddenly moved, conversing with a greyish haze at the Spirit Prison's edge.

He named the face she wore to fool others, "Mavis?"

Ryder's facial expression became bewildered as she listened in with her power of Telepathy. Using her power of Empathy, she accessed his body and was suddenly able to see the invisible woman standing there talking to him.

"Shut it," she growled, swiftly pointing her finger at him. "You're a snake. They are channeling the power of the Hellmouth. They are stronger and cleverer than I first realized. While the Modesto's conquer the bitches by abducting their precious Brady, I will find another way to defeat them. The hunters will become the hunted." She gave Sheppard a vision to pass onto their siblings. He was shown a glimpse of Jon Chasseur de Gitan, the Gypsy Hunter, coming to Treadwell. Mavis Romani a.k.a Morgana, gestured her hand and shoved it forward through the air at Sheppard, "Your sacrifice is not in vain, brother."

Unfreezing time...he was propelled backwards by her telekinesis.

Pilar, Juliann, Zane and Siobhan began to cast their spell again in Latin, "Secrets hide, rigid mind, open that, which is closed to mine." Sheppard broke out in manic laughter as he got up onto his feet again. Elevating their heads upward to the ceiling, the Romani chanted their spell louder, their voices stronger as they echoed. "Secrets hide!"

Turning around on the spot as he observed his siblings, Sheppard watched their eyes full of blue energy and then quickly it turned into impressive, scarlet flames as the Hellmouth yielded to them completely.

"We're the Triad," Pilar's voice was deep and fused with power, "telepathic and ultimate. Wielders of Nature. No mind is unreachable to us." Reaching her arm forward to Sheppard, she gestured her hand and twisted it in the air. "**OPEN!**" she commanded in a booming voice.

Sheppard buckled down onto his knees and clawed at his head as he cried out in excruciating pain.

~*~

Remaining in the Meat Locker, Avatarian Demigoddess Rafaela - dressed in a fanatical black satin gown adorned with overlapping pieces of emerald and purple lace - patiently waited for her mother, Alera, to complete her journey from the other side back to the world of the living via the mystical Phantom Mirror.

Impatiently, she observed the reflective surface. Behind her, trying to ignore it, the ethereal demigoddess could hear a conversation taking place.

"Be quiet you insolent ghoul," Rafaela spat irritably. Turning she was greeted by an empty altar, abandoned by Kamenwati. "What? Where the hell did she–" her words were cut short as a rift in the fabric of the dimension revealed the conversation taking place between Kamenwati, Isadora and Johdi Fox. "How," she spoke cautiously and with a hint of suspicion, "did they manage to capture–"

Abruptly, Kamenwati's body was ravished by flames and vanquished as she succumbed to her mortal wound. Bewildered at the defeat of her prized soldier, Rafaela's attention was promptly drawn to the cauldron bubbling away on the altar to the side of her. It exploded violently with a flash of light, quickly she shielded her face with her hands. Behind her came a sudden cracking noise. As though caught in slow motion, Rafaela turned just in time to witness the Phantom Mirror become consumed with cracks and then shatter into glittering pieces onto the ground before dissolving into dust. A side effect of Kamenwati being vanquished was, that what she conjured was destroyed along with her.

"NO!" she yelled frantically.

Suddenly, against her will, she was magically pulled into a whirlwind and then abruptly stopped by a man who grabbed her by her shoulders. Summoned to her own lair deep in the

Underworld, Asmodeus 'The Ancient and Great' Demon removed his hands from her slender frame as he stood bold in his charcoal business suit and styled salt and pepper hair.

"Asmodeus," her voice fled through her parted slips as she named him, "wh-what?"

His expressionless face did not show a sign of delight toward her. "Hello, Rafaela. It has been a while, since we saw one another. You've not aged a day, the centuries have been kind to you." Her lips curled at one end as though she smiled at the compliment even though he did not seem to be willing to show any sign of affection to couple the compliment given. "Your efforts to procure the Pogue Power appear somewhat dismal and the Duodecim are not happy."

She swayed uneasily as the two of them kept fierce eye contact.

"I will be taking over," he swiftly took her by the arm and threw her with little effort. She slammed against the massive window that overlooked the ocean floor and then fell onto the ground. "You were something to be marveled all those centuries ago. The Whore of Babylon. Now you're a little girl bent on conquests that are too big for you to achieve."

Rafaela levitated back up onto her feet and brushed the dirt from her gown. She moved the loose curls of hair from her face and expressed a very hostile glare as her eyes filled with black.

"All of this is mine." She placed her hands firmly on her hips in a pompous attempt to throw her weight and influence about. "You'd be proud of me, husband. I have conquered dimensions in your absence. I corrupted the king of the ocean. I–"

Asmodeus, outraged, cut her off. "I have no care for you and your idiot ego, Rafaela. That bitch, Connemara Preston, vanquished my lover Paimon and I intend on taking the battle to them."

Speechless for a moment, Rafaela blurted out, "You're gay?" In confusion.

"And you're a fanatical, spoilt brat!" he roared, swaying his arm and throwing her back against the window with his power of Telekinesis. "You've ignited battles that have left us with more causalities than victors. I visited your grandmother Uphara, and praised her the day she banished you from this world with the power of the moon. Bigger and better demons rose to the mantel of power and proved their worth."

Getting to her feet again, Rafaela spontaneously accelerated herself forward in a blurry streak of grey energy. Elevating his hand, he used his magic and caused her to slam against an invisible wall. Surprised by the sudden impact, her black and evil filled eyes became normal again. Swaying his hand again, he summoned a circle of white candles, trapping her in a Spirit Prison. Reaching her arm forward she let out a scream as the heat and light given off by the candles burnt her hand.

"Like I said," he folded his arms and a sly look on his face. "I intend on taking the battle to them. I've been orchestrating my plans from my icy prison for the past sixty years. And you've been none the wiser."

Rafaela, cradling her sore hand, listened to her ex-lover.

"You see," the smile lines in his smirk accentuated his smugness, "when it comes to you, Rafaela, I'm a little two-faced. I followed your mother, Alera, into battle. But you, I'd happily see dead. You only managed to procure a few secrets hidden inside Perry's nightmares that the Sognare Coven locked away through the aid of your puppet, Kamenwati." Her attention was suddenly drawn to a woman who looked awfully identical to Ravenna Straig as she emerged from Asmodeus' shadow on the left and Aaron Pogue emerging on the right. "While Paimon wanted his freedom from you and the Babylon Crystal you possessed, I had been in constant telepathic communication with these two as well as Astral Projecting."

Aaron spoke with overconfidence, "Do not be fooled by my appearance. My name is Razia and I have taken possession of this meat sack that you'd happily call, Aaron Pogue."

"We banished Aaron Pogue's soul into a mirror, trapping him in eternal limbo." The woman spoke equal egotism. "He is unable to die or move on." Rafaela stood silent, secretly impressed. "Tell us," the acid flowed over the woman's tongue as she addressed the demigoddess with a belittling attitude, "Rafaela, who has achieved more?"

Silence hugged Rafaela like a glove as she exchanged fiery glares with her new adversaries, while secretly using the power of empathy in her vast arsenal of powers to carefully look for a weakness in their bold pride. For the first time, her fate became clearer than clear as she realized that these three would end her life.

"I will pose as Aaron," Razia boasted. "Agreeing to return to the fold, I will have the brothers and I touch the Sundial and reactivate their broken power. There, I shall seize the opportunity to steal all their power and eradicate them and their line, once and for all."

A quiet Asmodeus suddenly interrupted, "And just like that, I established what has taken you far too long, Rafaela, to put in action."

The Ravenna look-alike blurted out arrogantly, "Any last words before we remove you from existence?"

With a brisk wave of his hand, Razia used telekinesis to throw Rafaela inside the Spirit Prison. The harsh impact against the invisible barrier broke her long gazelle horns - protruding from her forehead - near the base, leaving stubs of former beauty. Lying on the floor, a mortified Rafaela looked across the ground and acknowledged the pointed barbs that were once her horns. It was demoralizing, a queen, robbed of her crown and scepter. Flicking her eyes up from the ground she glared at her oppressors and her eyes filled with pitch black again. Accelerating with a blur back to her feet, Rafaela abruptly stopped still, her long hair in loose floating curls.

"If this is how it ends," her scolding glare could melt flesh from the bone, "so be it." Rigid in her movement, she reached her arms back and then drove them forward and yelled out in Latin, "Sacra speculum, frangit ieiunium (Sacred glass, shatter fast)."

The ocean beyond the magic fused glass groaned uneasily, dirt blew out from the rock-formed walls causing the woman to gasp and shield her face from the debris. Swiftly, splinters spread about the window and water began to spray into the lair.

Razia yelled in outrage, "YOU WILL KILL US ALL."

"I just did." Rafaela smirked confidently.

The ground felt like it suddenly dropped beneath their feet and another bold groan followed and the window gave way, shattering into a million pieces as the ocean poured in. Raising her hand to her lips she blew Asmodeus, Razia and the woman a kiss goodbye as she was swallowed by the body of water.

Chapter Nine

NEW DEMON ON THE BLOCK

Mother Nature began to manifest earlier than expected, during the month of April, as a Supercell Storm lashed Treadwell. Atop the mantle of the cloud mass - as it moved in over the city from the sea - stood a regal woman with long pastel pink hair that blew about in the gale-force wind.

"Behold the power of mother nature," she spoke with a South Carolina accent, her arms held out and her eyes were a glow with white light. "Upon the ocean my storm was called, onward to Treadwell, to make landfall." Pouring rain and gale force winds swept across the City Bound District of Treadwell. "Fear the rumbles, for I possess the power of thunder." An explosion tore across the sky. "In the dark, I light up the sky with a luminous spark." Flashes of lightning lit up the sky. "My mother, she named me, Evelina."

"Veniat ad me (Come to me)," a heavenly voice moved on the spirit wind. "Veniat ad me (Come to me), I call to thee, weather sprite."

Levitating with a stern look upon her face, the Tempo Being (Weather Sprite) glared down at the swaying surface of the clouds at her feet. Her eyes were full of glowing power while her long pink hair floated about. In a flash of light, she teleported to the individual that summoned her.

Mount Onóra and its lookout had the most spectacular, panoramic view of Treadwell along with its northern and southern suburbs. From here the sight of watching the Supercell Storm Evelina roll in over from the gulf was mesmeric, perhaps it was the way the rain swept across the mortal territory and the lightning hit the sea that made it breathtaking.

"*That which is bound to me.*" At the lookout, Persia Romani stood in the rain. Her magic protecting her as it pelted against an invisible force field. The wind swirled around her, blowing her clothes and long dark hair about. "*Veniat ad me (Come to me), to this place I be.*"

Opening her eyes quickly they met the Tempo Being's eyes like magnets.

"Hello mother." The pink haired sprite lowered her head respectfully as she levitated on the wind. "Does my storm blanket the city enough for you?" Twin brothers Mars and Dantalian stepped out of Persia's shadow, causing the creature to pause and then continue. "And your brothers to go undetected?"

Mars Romani, dapper and tall with a mop of blond hair complimented his sister, "I always admire your power to manipulate the weather and use it to cloak yourself. Mother will be pissed off to know we're home and not away at school."

Dantalian stood quiet with a stern look on his face as the heat from his powers of Pyrokinesis caused the air to ripple around him.

Persia smirked as she kept firm eye contact with the Sprite. "What she doesn't know won't hurt her." She then shifted her voice back toward Evelina. "Evelina, may I ask a favor of you?"

Evelina replied in a ghostly, echoing voice, "Ask and you shall receive, dearest."

"Are you able to locate a demon for me?" Persia looked hesitant.

The beautiful Sprite closed her eyes. A clap of thunder quickly followed and the twinkling, wet lights of the city below flickered and then became permanent again. She reopened her eyes.

"This city is riddled with evil," Evelina expressed obvious repulsion. "How does one survive it?"

Mars Romani a knowledgeable, know-it-all, spoke with self-assurance, "Because the city is built upon a Hellmouth, it inadvertently attracts all kinds. Except vampires, you will notice there is not or rarely a Vampire within Treadwell. There is enough good to protect it but the side of evil believe that with enough of it, they can corrupt the mystical hotspot and bring about an apocalypse."

Dismissing the male, Evelina addressed her conjurer, "Which location do you wish for me to divulge, Persia Romani?"

Mars and Persia both observed the windswept woman as she levitated in midair.

Persia smiled as the demon's name came to the front of her mind, "Find me the demon..." and there came a clap of thunder and as she listened to the Romani, Evelina the Weather Sprite nodded her head and then was gone in a flash of light.

~*~

In the pouring rain, the lights of the South Eastern Freeway had a supernatural glow. On the down track, two black SUVs approached the twin tube Hudson Tunnel. Atop the mountain that the tunnel went beneath, hidden amongst the gumtrees and invisible to mortals and most supernatural beings, was a gargantuan totem embellished with gold and copper colored hieroglyphs. It was the Deific that revealed herself to Johdi Fox in her native state. Sensing the vehicles that neared the tunnels below, the effigy gave off a glow and magically morphed into a gargantuan woman who knelt down on one knee.

"The way is closed," she said in an earth-shaking voice. "No passage for Vampires into Treadwell."

Using her infinite, divine power, the Deific activated the barrier of the Hellmouth beneath Treadwell. An invisible wall of energy glittered as the rain splattered against it. The unsuspecting vehicles, occupied by Vampires trying to enter the city were vaporized in brilliant rays of golden light and the cars reduced to piles of rust on the road.

On the side of the road, some distance away, an intimidated Caydit Packrem, Vampire Sovereign of Los Angeles observed as her minions tested the theory she had heard from demons back in the United States... *'The Hellmouth is heavily protected by good supernatural forces'.*

Caydit vanished in an accelerated blur and then reappeared at the pile of rust. Observing it, she turned her head slightly as a glitter of something drew her eyes to the first pile of rust a little further ahead of the one almost at her feet. Kneeling down she extended her arm forward. Behind her, the female Deific manifested, this time in a human sized form. Caydit stopped moving her arm forward for a moment as the little glittering-something became a rippling sheet of energy that divided her from the pile of rust.

"There is no passage," the Deific spoke, startling Caydit, causing her to stand up. "No passage is given to Vampires into Treadwell. I saw you in my thoughts before you decided to venture here." The Sovereign Vampire of Los Angeles remained silent as she listened and then her human visage morphed into a demon. "I name you, Cadán D'hôte... daughter of Esmeralda."

Looking over the holy woman, Caydit Packrem had long gone by the name Caydit or Cayden; no one living new her proper birth name, Cadán D'hôte. Fearing the fate that would become of her, similar to that of her minions who'd just perished, the Vampire Sovereign vanished in an accelerated blur, disappearing into the country town of Lorri that was close by. *It was proclaimed by the Deific who revealed herself to Johdi Fox that they manifested in this world between the departure of the Old Ones and the rise of the Divine Beings. While one governs the Hellmouth and Treadwell, another gargantuan totem embellished with gold and copper colored hieroglyphs governs Vancouver from its hidden sanctuary of Stanley Park, another in Central Park, New York.*

~*~

At 60-62 Grevillea Way, Chickerell Creek - east of Treadwell in the Rune Mountains - the rain continued to pour as the wind blew through the tall hedge that acted as the front fence of Noah Pogue's two storey house. The wet foliage glimmered under the street lights as they swayed energetically. Thunder rumbled in the greyish-purple storm clouds as an array of lightning forked across the night sky.

"I find," Perry's voice moved about the attic, filled with warm golden light, "it hard to comprehend that you vanquished Kamenwati." Looking up from the family's Book of Shadows he observed his cousin as she picked up the candles that littered the floor. "How is that possible? I would have thought the power of four witches could vanquish her. Like any other Superior Level Demon."

Johdi's eyes caught Perry's as she knelt down and then rose up. "I am an adept witch, cousin." She wasn't egotistic in her self-assurance but confident enough in her own independence. "Who said anything about the power of four witches being required to vanquish Kamenwati? I merely weakened her by manipulating her fears and killed her with them."

Isadora interrupted, "Of all things, being mortal and dying like one was her ultimate fear. That was how Johdi weakened her for me to be able to wound her with one of my Light Darts."

Noah, reading a book on the old sofa to the side of the room, looked up and spoke with confusion. "I believe Johdi has more than enough power and combined with Isadora's, they were able to vanquish Kamenwati. But what I find most intriguing," he lent his hands across the open book in his lap, "you met a, Deific."

Johdi didn't share the same enthusiasm. "Yeah, you see," sarcasm was almost evident in her voice as she gestured a hand in the air, "when you meet someone or something you know nothing about, nor knew existed, it kind of puts you a little on edge. For all I knew she could have been a minion of Rafaela's or fanatic follower of the evil Old One, Eisheth."

Noah smirked as he observed her. "You're a Pogue, last name or not. You're caution is your greatest asset."

Johdi smiled in Noah's direction.

Perry appeared a bit perplexed. "I would have said highly judgmental. But you're words seemed nicer than mine."

Johdi then shot a cold glare in the opposite direction at Perry.

"This world and the Supernatural one have secrets," Noah began, rising from the sofa with the book open in his hands. "Secrets people take to their graves, societies, etc." Unseen by the occupants in the room, an apparition of Aaron Pogue manifested in the mirror on the wall and then quickly disappeared. "There are lots of secret magics," as he closed the book and put it down on the sofa Noah gestured his fingers to make a quotation, "'in our' world that we still don't know enough about to utilize. The Deific, are an example of that. From my recollection when the Old Ones left this world and before the Deities rose to power in Egypt, the Deific nurtured earth back to a paradise. They established Babylon. In some circles it is said, that the Deific are related to the Whale-Mouth Leviathan-"

Isadora blurted out in confusion, "Hellmouths?"

"Also known as, Hellmouths," Noah exchanged a stare with Isadora as he gestured his hand at her before continuing. "These godly giants in their natural state appear as gargantuan totems embellished with gold and copper colored hieroglyphs. Their magic is tied to the Hellmouth, if a Deific falls; the Hellmouth becomes compromised, vulnerable to evil."

"This one seemed very prophetic," Johdi remarked vaguely. "She said that vanquishing Kamenwati would not prevent tomorrow's problem that lingered in the mirror."

Isadora spoke for a moment, "So in my head this theory makes sense, not sure if it will come out the same way." Noah, Perry and Johdi listened with careful eyes. "The Deific are like a weir gate? When there is too much water, water being all that is evil in Treadwell, the weir gate becomes compromised and can buckle?"

Perry nodded his head silently as he made sense of what she said.

"I guess. If you put it that way," Noah in a way, agreed. "You will never find Vampires near in a city built on a Hellmouth." Isadora and Johdi made odd expressions as they both looked from Noah to Perry. Noah continued, "It's because the Hellmouth is pure magical, celestial energy. Technically a vampire is someone who has died. Therefore being soulless corrupts positive forces."

Isadora couldn't make head-or-tail of the sudden revelation, "So what about the entire Underworld beneath Treadwell?"

"Vampire's exist above ground, they do not linger beneath and then manifest within the city like demons do. Vampires have and always will be an exiled creature, outlaws. They reside in cities that aren't protected by magic, like Los Angeles. Caydit Packrem has significant sovereignty there because she has no disadvantage like she would have here. This is consecrated ground. Perry," Noah gestured his hand at his brother, "is only half Vampire, still very much a living, breathing human being and a powerful witch. He is what I call a Nefas. The Deific views him as possessing a soul. But in regards to your question about every other demon that lurks here, good and evil are bound to one another. It's the order of everything. It's all balanced according to the Grand Design that governs everything including Hellmouths and The Deific."

There came a sudden noise-like a clap of thunder and an explosion of energy mixed with white lightning at the center of the room. As he manifested, Asmodeus, cast out a pulse of energy. Letting out a scream, Johdi was blown away to the side of the attic. Forcibly she slammed into a cupboard. Perry was thrown backwards and Noah somersaulted through the air, crashed back into the sofa he sat upon, flipping it over and tumbling onto the floor.

To the side of the demon, just out of arm's length, Isadora stood unaffected. Her power of Energy Manipulation granted her certain immunities to energy-based powers and attacks.

"So," Asmodeus' voice was deep, charming and somewhat disappointed, "is this all that stands to guard the Hellmouth? The prominent Pogue Witches." He observed the two brothers as they clambered up onto their feet. "I was expecting," turning his head he admired Isadora as she stood still, "more... aren't you a vision." He gave her a wink. "You remind me of Saturn-"

A cautious Isadora looked at him and then over at Noah for clarification.

Asmodeus eyeballed Noah, "You don't know me. But me and those who I represent know all there is to know about you, Noah Pogue." Looking at the two men, Asmodeus told the truth, strange, even for a demon. "I was expecting four siblings. Not two brothers, a niece and a ring-in."

Emerging at his other side, fiery Johdi, her aura and eyes consumed with red energy from her power of Fear Inducement, swiftly swayed her right gestured hand. A bolt of red energy hit Asmodeus.

"I am hardly a ring-in-" her words were brief.

Opening his hand, Asmodeus removed the red energy from his body into his hand and then threw it back at her, launching her back across the room. This time she slammed into the wall, knocking her out cold.

He huffed confidently, "I am not just your common demon, witch."

Growling, Perry's face morphed into his vampire form. Responding on pure instinct instead of caution and logic, he accelerated himself in a blur across the room. Stopping instantly he swung a punch, striking Asmodeus across the face. A second round had the demon grab Perry's hand, twist his arm and then head butt him. With a swish of his free hand, the man dressed in a tailor-made, designer suit used his powers to break his opponent knees. Letting out an intense cry of pain Perry began to drop toward the floor.

"You are nothing without your united power." Asmodeus growled as he glared into Perry's green eyes. "If you're going to oppose me and the Disciples then expect imminent death. I will break you the same way I broke Rafaela's horns," and then he proceeded to briskly snap Perry's neck, killing him.

Hastily moving his hands away from the families Book of Shadows, Perry gasped slightly as he returned from his premonition and acknowledged the page he had been resting on as being the one titled, Asmodeus. He failed to realize that it was the same demon that he and Noah had encountered in the Botanical Gardens while in the company of Serene and Madelyn Romani.

Reengaging the conversation around him, Perry spat sarcastically, "So this entire time were you researching that demon we encountered or were you just polishing your Custodian knowledge?"

A concerned Johdi queried, "What demon?"

Perry replied, "Asmodeus."

Outside in the street, under the cloak of pouring rain, a black sedan pulled up to the curb and the occupant observed Noah's house behind the towering front hedge. Lowering the passenger side window, Aaron Pogue revealed himself.

SOMETHING SECRET – PART ONE

I t was 90's week in Treadwell's trendy, retro, Levu nightclub.

Tonight the girl band named, Sorority - to the supernatural world, they were the Siren Sorority - performed. In the darkness electric guitars played, drums pounded and then in quick flashes of light each individual girl was shown on the circle stag in the clubs center.

Leader of the group, Louisiana Pratt, yelled out a countdown as they began their rendition of Janet Jackson's rock-pop song 'Black Cat'.

The Siren Sorority, were an inspiring act of feminism. A group of strong, supernatural assassins individualized by fantastic hairstyles and colors, but united in their extroverted attitude 'eye for an eye, tooth for a tooth' and their seductive attires. Any demon or evil entity that had deliberately or accidently gone up against them did not live long enough to sing a fable about them.

~*~

Months prior...

P owerful illusionist witch, Connemara Penthal, had been rescued from the clutches of Sabar, the Sabarticar Demon at Butchard Garden near Victoria, British Columbia, Canada from

Sorority member, Rubella. Transported to Siren Headquarters, Connemara was forced to adjust to life under witness protection.

Lark Eavan with her beautiful pink hair done in curls, sat opposite the witch in the main atrium with her legs crossed. "The place is fused with magic, so you, witchy-pooh, are unable to escape. So no funny business," she waved her hands at Connemara vaguely, "with your wicked illusion powers."

Her teal colored eyes attracted Connemara's.

"I still do not understand why I am here," the witch protested.

Lark spoke again, "The entire place is a Spirit Prison. No one can, literally sense you here. Only us." She smirked, pleased with the result. "You've been naughty-"

Maria's voice interrupted, "You may go, Lark, I will speak with the witch." The Siren and the Old One exchanged a stare upon the superior power entering the room. Lark swiftly vanished in a gleam of pink light. "Connor."

Sitting in the white leather armchair, Connemara did not turn to acknowledge her superior, instead trembled a little at the thought of being in the presence of the queen of magic. Maria was graceful as she seemed to levitate across the floor dressed in a grey knitted dress, a long sleeve maroon-colored cardigan that draped down on the floor and gathered around the heels of her knee-high brown suede boots.

Her long brunette hair, styled in stylish curls, fell down past her shoulders with some gathered in a messy bun at the back.

"My friend." Maria smiled as she halted in front of the witch. "It has been a while since we last saw one another." Connemara rose from her seat and they exchanged a hug before they both sat again. "The reasons for you being here belong to the G.S.B. You're one of the Bureau's best agents and witch. But concerns have arisen. The magic you put in place to protect the Pogue Family has begun to fail."

Emotion rose to the surface of Connemara's face, "I-I need to go and protect my-"

Maria raised her hand to her friend. "I cannot allow that, Connor. Not now. It's too dangerous. We don't know how, but your position in Rafaela's circle may have become compromised. It was sheer luck that the descendants from your first life have lived this long."

Connemara protested irritably, "And how many times do you want me to apologize for being evil in a past life? So far, I think I am up too one-thousand. The CEO was just fortunate that Connemara Preston and I are identical in appearance for me to vanquish her and assume her identity."

~*~

Patrons danced about the floor in Levu as the Siren Sorority continued to perform on stage. Hidden amongst the mortals, Persia Romani, held her arms up in the air, swaying them about as she twirled around. At the bar, Dantalian Romani and his brother Mars waited for two bottles of beer. Turning his head, as he leaned against the modern bar, Mars caught a glimpse of Aaron Pogue as he stood at the end, chitchatting with a woman as they drank their beverages.

"I did not realize," Mars leant close to Dan's ear as he spoke loudly, "Mr. Pogue ventured to bars." Dan turned as they both observed Aaron. "Do you think his wife knows?" Their eyes widened with surprise as they witnessed him kiss the lady on the neck.

~*~

*M*aria spoke again, gentle in nature, "And we thank you for that. But there is a problem. Rafaela is not the only superior, evil force active in Treadwell anymore. There's a new player in town. Lurking in the shadows and pulling strings." Connemara and she exchanged a nervous stare. "What do you know?"

Connemara appeared smug. "I know plenty of things."

Maria's eyes turned from humble brown to electric blue and her brown hair turned brown to platinum blonde. "You know better than to play games with me, Connemara Penthal." In a burst of black smoke, she altered the witches form from human to a crow and then human again. "What is it we're dealing with?"

An intimidated Connemara replied, "You already know who the threat is. In the place that even darkness fears, who lingers." Listening to the witch as Maria's visage relaxed, they both said at the same time, "The Twelve Disciples." There came an uncomfortable silence. "The Potentate reached Malice, making her the first evil witch. During the time of Babylon, the Disciples reached Alera via Asmodeus, turning a powerful Stealth Witch against her sister Lindsay and mother Uphara."

Maria blurted out, "But Asmodeus was entombed in ice by the goddess Rhea."

Connemara showed a look of knowing. "I vanquished the demon Paimon. He was the front man for the Disciples. And Rhea had it that as long as one lived, the other would remain frozen. Until such time as one was vanquished, only then would Asmodeus be freed. So the thing behind the curtain is-"

Maria realized, "Asmodeus."

~*~

Turning his back, Dantalian promptly took Mars by the hand activating their triplet power. Magically he was able to Astral Project himself to the other end of the bar and was invisible to Aaron as he stepped out from behind his right shoulder to admire and observe the beautiful young woman he flirted with that was not his wife, Ravenna.

"Mars," Dan spoke, revealing what he could see. "This woman is a witch."

Looking around to see if anyone was watching, Mars then looked back at his brother. "What do you mean she's a witch?" His eyes moved from left to right as he observed Dan's. "How can you tell?"

Dan stepped around the woman as she sat on the barstool. "She possesses a talisman around her neck. Why would-" turning his head as he acknowledged Aaron, Dan noticed something unusual about the eldest Pogue brother. "How odd, his aura is black..." gasping he returned to his body. Dan turned his head slightly as he engaged Mars. "Something," turning a little more he looked back down the bar and noticed the suddenly vacant space that Aaron and the woman once occupied, "something is not right, we need to find Persia." He and Mars exchanged a serious stare. "Fast."

On stage, the Siren Sorority too were observing Aaron from the seclusion of the stage. Sensing the use of magic in Levu, they all swiftly put their eyes upon the two Romani standing at the bar.

Sensing the sudden attention, Mars looked out the corner of his eye. "Dan, we've been found out."

~*~

"*When I occupied a seat in Rafaela's court,*" Connemara rose from the white leather armchair and walked around behind it, "*there was talk that she was supposed to free the Disciples with the power of the Hellmouth. But instead turned against them to fulfil her own desire to rule the Underworld and use the power of the Hellmouth to resurrect Alera. She informed Saxon Preston, Riley Preston and me, her precious Trinity, that her efforts to conquer Treadwell were deemed dismal and that her superior, Paimon, had warned her that she'd be removed if she did not improve.*"

Maria spoke again, "Rafaela's efforts have been successful. She had Nightmare Soldier, Kamenwati, abduct Perry and remove his nightmares. Now a Laedo has both him and Noah." Connemara suddenly appeared uneasy. "*I had to secretly encourage Bermuda and Isadora to travel to Canada to team up with Andromeda. The three of them together can channel enough power to access the Dream World.*"

Connemara's voice was shaky, "No, Maria, You don't understand. You said a Laedo. You even said that the Oracles of Phaedra foresaw that a Laedo would enter the Pogue Circle and that they would not know the difference because it possessed a familiar guise." Maria rose from her seat with a nervous look on her face. "*You don't need my daughters. You need Aaron to restore-*"

Suddenly, Maria swayed her arm out and gestured her hand, rendering Connemara unconscious as she fell to the floor.

"*Thanks, you've been a pal,*" Maria spoke arrogantly, her aura shone for a second and Asmodeus resumed his male visage. "*I now know how to infiltrate the Pogue Coven.*" In a flash of lightning and pulse of energy she teleported out.

~*~

On stage, the hands of the Siren Sorority were drawn to one another like magnets and clamped together. Pink magical energy shone in their eyes and they used their combined power of Eloquence to stop time and freeze all the mortals within Levu.

Dancing around on the spot, Persia accidently bumped into a stiff figure. It was then she immediately realized that someone had used magic.

"What the?" she muttered to herself, staggering about as she observed all the other mortals. "Mars, Dan." Turning around she was greeted by a highly pissed off Louisiana Pratt, leader of the Sorority. "Whoa."

Louisiana growled, "Hello, Persia Romani." Her eyes glowing with fierce pink energy. "Care to explain why you and your kind are using magic so carelessly in our club?" Swiftly, Persia turned her head and saw her twin brothers standing at the bar, guarded by two Sirens. "Well go on, speak, you've risked exposing us all."

Mars spoke up, "We're tracking a demon."

Louisiana looked at him and then back at Persia, "There are no demons here. And if there were, we'd know before you would. Considering how significantly more powerful we are to you." Persia suddenly became smug and her body language confrontational. "Get out of our club."

With a swift hand gesture, Persia made quick bolts of lightning strike the floor in-between the mortals around her, promptly missing them. Her long hair suddenly blew about in a magical wind. Instinctively, Louisiana took a step backward as she both sensed the escalation in the Romani's power and received visions of the Old One, The Morrígan.

Mars and Dan whispered to their sister telepathically, "The demon left."

Persia's eyes gave off a subtle shine. "We'll show ourselves out."

~*~

*R*eappearing, in another pulse of energy and flash of lightning,

Asmodeus manifested in a ghostly cemetery filled with low fog and the full moon high in the black, starry sky. With a brisk sway of his arm and gesture of his hand he used his demonic powers to summon two heavily cloaked individuals to his location.

"My lord," said one in heavenly voice.

The other just stood there, showing no respect. With another sway of his hand he made their baggy attire disappear in glows of light, revealing Ravenna, the wife of Aaron Pogue and her sister Rasima Straig.

"I have an assignment." He stood poised in his tailored, designer suit. "You two are to lure Aaron Pogue into a trap. Expel him from his body and take possession of it."

Ravenna, an unhinged psychopath, but easily camouflaged, smirked as she spoke. "He is an idiot, my lord. A fool, he is to relinquish his magic." She spoke sarcastically, "Wishing it away because he deemed it too dangerous because it killed mummy dearest. Aaron believes it will only result in the deaths of his loved ones."

Rasima stepped forward, her long black hair blew in the sudden wind. "My lord, we shall do as you have asked. I am the Laedo of the two, more powerful. Forgive my sister, as a younger woman she suffered a mental breakdown. Seductively psychotic she is that is why she was born under the Gemini star sign. Split

112

personality. She has played the perfect role of innocent wife for so long that the Pogue Witches would not see her betrayal coming until death itself broke down the door."

Asmodeus smiled, satisfied. "I like death. Death is good."

~*~

The rain continued to fall as the storm, named Evelina that Persia Romani conjured, continued to loom over half of Deane County and Treadwell City. Street lights had a supernatural aura that lined Hemming Way. Opposite Levu, the wet leaves of the tall trees that adorned Cotton Park glimmered in the light. The sound of splashing water left little silence as traffic moved on the city streets.

Atop her plateau, Evelina, with her long pink hair flapping in the gale-force winds, waved her hand out in front of her making the cloud surface ripple like water. Using the power of Voyeurism, she observed Aaron Pogue and his date walk along the city street.

"Veniat ad me (Come to me)," a heavenly voice moved on the spirit wind.

Evelina looked up and away from her viewing pond as she acknowledged the call.

"Veniat ad me (Come to me)," the voice moved again, "Evelina."

Standing beneath the trees of Cotton Park, Persia, Mars and Dantalian held hands; their eyes closed and they used their combined power to summon Evelina to their location. Before them, an abrupt wind blew up and in a flash of pink light, the Weather Being manifested. She levitated a few inches above the wet grass.

The trio opened their eyes.

"Were you able to track him?" Persia queried,

Evelina silently nodded her head and then spoke, "Yes, my liege. He bares the stench of something rotted through, something that should not belong to someone like him. If you say he is a good witch." The Romani triplets silently listened to the magical woman talk. "He," she closed her eyes and used the storm overhead to look down upon Treadwell to track Aaron Pogue's movements. "He walks with a woman south from here, just a minutes' walk into the park," her voice dropped as though miserable. "I am unable to follow him, my liege by sky. The trees of Cotton Park, they help him hide from my eyes."

Persia sighed at the misfortune, "Thank you Evelina. You may go now."

Magically released from the beautiful Romani, Evelina nodded her head and vanished in another flash of pink light. Disappointed but not discouraged, Mars began to move about, running his hands across the tree trunks and then stopped, turned and beamed an ideal smile at his twin siblings.

"Mother would kill us," he expressed a ploy with a sly approach, "but we, you," he pointed at Dan, "we," he then pointed to Persia, "us." He placed his hand on his chest. "We're the Morrígan. The Old One reincarnated in the form of three Mischling. In our slumber, in the Dream World we are that, but what if we-"

A cautious Dantalian protested, "I don't like where this is going. We risk a hell of a lot by doing that. We could die using that kind of power."

"As long as we're separated, The Morrígan can only exist in the Dream World." Persia too sounded hesitant. "Accessing our full power as one, we risk releasing it back into this world. I enjoy being me; I do not wish to be taken over by an uncontrollable alter-ego, Mars."

Dan protested again, "What if someone sees us, Mars."

"Iungo. (Connect)" Mars held his hand and commanded arrogantly in Latin. Suddenly, by magic, Persia and Dan gasped as they were pulled to their brother and hands clasped together. "We find him my way." And with his free hand, Mars planted it against the tree. "Travel tall, seeing all, trees in nature, open doors." Casting his spell, "Take us to where this evil dwells." Spontaneous green energy glowed from his and then abruptly the three siblings disappeared into the tree, using it as a portal.

SOMETHING SECRET – PART TWO

*R*avenna, Rasima and Aaron Pogue sat at the dining table enjoying a home-cooked meal. The gentle white light of the crystal chandelier glimmered in their eyes as they smiled, ate and conversed with one another.

"Oh sister," Ravenna portrayed excitement, "it is wonderful to have you back in Treadwell after such a long time abroad."

Rasima took a sip of her red wine. "I have missed you too, sister."

"Please," Aaron spoke as he wiped his mouth, "please excuse me. I suddenly do not feel so good. I think I need a glass of water." He rose from his seat, and the two sisters watched him at first with considerate eyes but the moment he turned his back, their eyes filled with evil. "Continue without me."

Walking away from the table, Aaron stumbled and then collapsed, knocking a chair over and pulling the tablecloth down to the floor along with the dinner plates, food and wine flutes. A cautious Ravenna and Rasima slowly rose from their seats as they observed the unconscious Aaron as he lay on the floor. Turning their heads, they smiled upon one another. Their plan to subdue him had worked, now they had to expel him from his body so Rasima could possess it.

In the attic of Aaron Pogue's Summit Hills, two storey home; Ravenna and Rasima had laid Aaron on the floor inside a Spirit Prison and instead of creating it out of the usual white candles, they had created an evil version by the use of black ones with grey flames.

"Inside out, outside in, in this body, a soul does swim, expel the good," together, hand in hand, the two sisters cast their evil spell in unison, "and replace with sin."

Feeling the instant effects of the spell, Rasima elevated her face, with her eyes closed, toward the ceiling and let out a gasp with an evil, humble smile. Spontaneously her body collapsed into black smoke and she was whisked away into the Spirit Prison.

"With spell," Ravenna continued as her voice echoed and was full of power, "swap his place."

White ghostly energy escaped his body and promptly Rasima entered, taking possession of the male body. Taking a human form that levitated at the circle's edge, Aaron's spirit appeared startled at the revelations. He watched his body awaken and then climb up onto its feet. Turning, Aaron's two faces met one another. Magically, the outline of the physical form shone and then shapeshifted into Rasima.

"What have you done?" Aaron's ghostly voice echoed.

Rasima replied humbly, "Getting rid of you." Swiftly extending her arm at him, she used her evil powers to propel his spirit backward toward the mirror mounted on the wall behind him. "Into the void, the secret space where no one shall look or see your face." The reflective surface of the mirror gave off a glow as Aaron's spirit was absorbed into it. Waving her hand across her face, she shapeshifted back into Aaron's form and bragged, "Look at how easy it was to infiltrate the Pogue Coven. I will convince them that I want to reunite and be a witch again. Once we've reconstituted your families' powerful magic, Asmodeus will use it to corrupt the Hellmouth and free the Disciples. Something that insolent Rafaela has failed to do."

~*~

In the front yard of Aaron Pogue's, Summit Hills, property one of the three tree trunks gave off a brilliant green glow as an accelerated blur fled it and Mars, Persia and Dantalian manifested. Dumbfounded, the spell that was supposed to take them to Aaron Pogue in Cotton Park had mysteriously taken them to a place he had once lived, that unbeknownst to them, was now owned by Estia Bradmore.

"What the f-" Persia blurted out in a fit of confusion.

Emerging out of the shadows of the trees, Louisiana Pratt lowered her hand as it glowed with mystical purple glowing energy. She had manipulated the Romani's spell to use the trees as a form of travel, redirecting to another location instead so that she and her group of hit-women could procure Aaron himself.

Lark Eavan appeared over her shoulder. "Are you sure you want to do this?"

Louisiana Pratt extinguished her power as she glared ahead into the parklands. "The assignment was to procure the witch who is without magic. The Romani Triplets I had not foreseen as being involved. The Oracles of Phaedra are concerned that a demon has infiltrated the Pogue Coven and that is what we need to prevent."

The arrogance of power made the Siren Sorority powerful but also perhaps allowed them to be blindsided as well. It was this arrogance and seducing foes to their death that had Sabar, The Sabarticar Demon, hunt and murder them.

"Come," she said in a low tone, "he is that way." Louisiana pointed her hand ahead of herself as she sensed Aaron's presence and together they proceeded onwards into the rainy night across Cotton Park.

Poor light shone through the foliage and cast a silhouette across Ravenna's face as she knelt down beside the witch she had seduced in Levu and was going to kill in cold blood.

"Please," the woman whimpered, unable to move. "Please don't kill me."

Ravenna caressed the woman's forehead. "Shh." She subdued the fear and emotion in her victim. "It will only hurt for a minute." Promptly she raised her hand into the air, revealed her Athame and then drove it into the woman's abdomen as she smothered her scream of agony with her hand. "Death comes to all witches. It would be wrong to assume you're excused from it." Relinquishing her magic to Ravenna, the innocent woman's power of Deflection glowed as it was absorbed into the knife and then into the evil witch's hand. "Disperse," she commanded, swaying her hand over the dead witch, making her lifeless body scatter into molecules.

"Do you remember the plan?" Aaron, possessed by Rasima, stepped into view of Ravenna as she knelt in the grass.

Rising up, Ravenna's body altered and grew in height as she shapeshifted into Aaron Pogue. Her long black, platted hair became blonde and shaggy, while her brown eyes turned amber. Both versions of Aaron smiled at one another. Waving his hand past his face, the version possessed by Rasima gained cuts, bruises and abrasions to his body, a facade to make it look as though he had been attacked.

"Go to the witches," the version of Aaron, concealing Ravenna's identity, gave the other instructions. "Play to their decent nature. You were attacked by one of Rafaela's minions and your wife is missing. That you've decided to take back your magic and insist that reuniting your power to take down Rafaela is the only option."

Nodding his head, Aaron/Rasima vanished in a burst of black smoke.

Suddenly, Aaron/Ravenna's attention was drawn by the snapping sound of a twig. Emerging out from behind the trees and shadows, a group of women had circled the witch they were sent to procure. Louisiana Pratt moved forward toward the person she believed was Aaron Pogue.

"Aaron Pogue," she addressed him, her beauty mesmerized him, created a foggy sensation around his head. "I am Louisiana Pratt. This is the Siren Sorority. We've been requested to take you into our protective custody."

Both of them exchanged an enthralled stare.

Knocking on the front door of Aaron Pogue's house, Persia, Mars and Dan were greeted by a woman dressed in a nightgown.

"Hello," she greeted the three Romani. "Can I help you?"

Persia muttered awkwardly, "Oh. Doesn't Aaron Pogue live here?"

The woman replied, "No sorry, he doesn't. I am Estia Bradmore. I just recently purchased the house."

~*~

"**W**hat do we know," Johdi Fox continued the conversation in the attic of Noah's house with him, Perry and Isadora, "about this Asmodeus?"

The room was full of warmth and golden light. At the windows, rumbles of thunder rattled, rain lashed against them as lightning flashed behind the clouds. Evelina, the Weather Being, was putting on a mild display compared to the storm, named Séverine, that had blanketed Treadwell, leaving much destruction in her path some many months ago. At the door, one of Isadora's sons had appeared dressed in his little pajamas and holding his medium-sized plush giraffe by the leg; its head dragging on the floor behind him.

"Mama," he summoned her in his small voice.

Turning her head, Isadora brushed some of her long auburn hair away from her face and gasped a little with concern. Looking back at her elders, she raised her index finger.

"Excuse me, one of my little persons is at the door," and quickly she moved toward the door. Gently ushering him out of the doorway, she closed the door behind her and knelt down to his level. "Owen, what are you doing out of bed? Did you have a bad dream? Do you need to go to the toilet?"

His little eyes were magnetized to her indigo colored ones.

"I had a dream, mama," he revealed his power of Dream Precognition.

She sympathized and swooped him up into her arms and rose, kissing him on the forehead. Walking away to the left of the attic door, she began the journey of the usual stop at the bathroom door in case he needed to pee before returning to bed. His giraffe dangled at Isadora's side as she walked down the hallway. Halting suddenly, her attention was caught by a thunderous knocking on the front door downstairs. For a moment she wasn't sure if she had mistaken the sound for the thunder outside but then it came again.

Startled, Owen gasped and panicked in his mother's grasp. "The man, mama. He is here." Isadora patted her sons golden blond hair as she looked down the staircase and then turned and looked over her shoulder at the half closed attic door. "Mama."

"Shh, it's okay baby," she comforted her child. "NOAH. PERRY, there is someone at the front door."

The door sprang open; Noah came out first, then Perry and then finally Johdi.

To describe Noah Pogue's house from the outside one would say it was a plain rectangle two storey abode. When he and his high school sweetheart, Connemara Penthal, drew up their own floor plans they wanted a large lounge space in the front left section that filtered in a lot of natural light, tall ceilings and a Canadian inspired fireplace. In the middle a large circle foyer/main entry into the home with a mesmerizing staircase that curved around the room to the right, up to the second floor. To the right, through timber french doors with fogged glass inserts would be the home office come library. The lounge and circular foyer connected to the back of the house through square archways. Between the foyer and the gourmet kitchen in the back was a powder room, mudroom and laundry.

Enchanted with a combination of Noah and Connemara's powerful magic, the front mortal world, Chickerell Creek entrance was different to the view in the rear. The secret to the home was that it bordered two dimensions. The dining room, kitchen and small lounge area - designed and decorated with large ceiling to floor, iron sculpted windows, dark, polished timber floor boards and chandeliers that resembled antlers with light bulbs - looked out into a cottage garden that lined a cobble street in the good-witch-only pocket dimension referred to as either 'The Grove' or 'New Salem'. A modern New York meets medieval Paris, both creatively woven together to establish a cultured city that was impenetrable to evil while it hid and protected good witches. It was created by Maria during the Salem Witch Hunts.

On the Chickerell Creek side of the house, the roof was green and corrugated with a modern, rendered street appeal. The Grove side of the house was a gorgeous British inspired country cottage with a thatched roof and stone wall structure.

Hurrying down the staircase, Noah reached the modern front doors. Perry stood on the last step of the stairs while Johdi stood out in the middle of the foyer between the two brothers with a firm territorial look set in her face. Above on the top of the staircase, Isadora had a prime view of the happenings below.

"Demons don't usually knock," Perry cautioned sarcastically.

Johdi moved her head as she listened and agreed. Taking the door handle in his hand, Noah turned it and then pulled the door open and to his startled expression he was greeted by a beaten and wet Aaron Pogue.

Isadora, shocked, accidently blurted out, "Oh my god."

Johdi and Perry stood with their eyes wide in disbelief while Noah remained speechless as his older brother held himself up by leaning against the doorframe.

"The," Aaron coughed, his wet blond hair clung to his face, "Prodigal brother returns." He brushed his fringe from his eyes. "Are you going to welcome me into your house, brother?"

Invisible to the witches' eyes and beyond the comprehension of their supernatural senses, Old One, Vesta, permanently possessing the body of the Filipino Witch, Aryan, stood in the middle of the foyer and observed. Her presence completely unfelt, but her eyes filled with ridicule toward the witches for letting Aaron into the house as she stood with her arms folded firmly.

Raising her hand up beside her head, Aryan swiftly gestured it as she spoke in Latin, "Patet (manifest)" and like a broken water main that everyone could see, spontaneous white smoke burst up from the floor and dark haired Custodian, Pridham, appeared in the house. Collapsing toward the floor, Noah went to catch his older brother.

Aryan murmured in a firm tone, "Don't let them touch him."

Pridham gasped, reaching her arm out in front. "Don't touch him." And with a brisk flick of the wrist she made Aaron magically vanish in a rush of white smoke and then, through the doorway to the right, he reappeared in another burst of smoke where he collapsed onto the sofa. Noah, Johdi and Perry acknowledged the brazen Custodian with absurd looks. "I will heal him."

Noah slammed the front door shut. "Are you kidding me?" Outrage evident in his voice.

Confused, Perry queried bluntly, "Who the hell are you?"

Noah turned and glared at Pridham. "So you think it's alright that you waltz into my house," the four of them began to walk into the other room, "and dictate to me how to aid my brother?" Their voices became inaudible to Isadora at the top of the stairs.

"Isadora..." a ghostly voice licked up the back of Isadora's neck, "Isadora..."

Gasping suddenly, she looked at her son again. "Owen?" believing that it was him who had said her name. "Okay. Time I put you back to bed." Walking away from the staircase, Isadora ventured off down the hallway toward a bedroom with a door half open and partly lit by the glow of a small lamp.

"Save me..." whispered the voice again.

The door to the attic creaked as it slowly opened on its own. Closing the bedroom door after returning her son to bed, Isadora approached the staircase. This time an uncomfortable feeling set in as a silhouette of someone walking about the empty and well-lit room drew her attention. An icy chill ran up her spin as she froze in fear. Against her better judgement, she took a deep breath and began to approach the attic door. Stopping at it, she cautiously pushed it open a little further until it was fully open.

"Hello?" she queried aloud.

Nervously, she looked about the room from the doorway and then decided to enter, holding her hand open at her side she began to gather photons into her open palm in anticipation of having to use her power of Photokinesis to defend herself. Entering into the empty and silent room, she approached the center of the room where the partially dismantled Spirit Prison was. Behind her,

124

on the sofa where Noah had sat, a figure sat in silence as it observed the witch as she stood with her back to it. Isadora glanced about the room cautiously until another icy chill ran up her neck. Gasping she glanced out the corner of her eye at the sofa behind her. Nothing was there. It was empty.

Returning her attention to the room before her, she let out a slight shriek as a hornless Rafaela stood before her in a torn, ruined and damp gown. The attic door slammed shut.

"I need your help."

Snapping her fingers she used magic to render Isadora unconscious on the floor.

Chapter Twelve

DESPERATE MEASURES

*K*neeling down on the floor beside the sofa, Pridham moved her hands out over the abrasions on Aaron's chest and head. She observed him with concerned and caring eyes. Closing them, she elevated her face toward the ceiling, murmured a prayer and spontaneously her hands began to give off an amethyst glow as they began to heal the witch. Noah stood just behind Pridham's shoulder, Johdi at the end of the sofa while Perry stood back, occupying the space in the doorway. He wasn't entirely convinced. Suddenly, moving uneasily, his vampire senses took notice of a creaking noise of the attic door. Perry turned his head and elevated his eyes upward toward the ceiling.

"Did you hear that?" he queried.

Johdi, paying more attention to Aaron awakening on the lounge replied, "Hear what?" her voice laced with confusion. "I didn't hear anything."

Noah observed Aaron with his curious blue sapphire eyes as Pridham withdrew her hands and then rose up beside her fellow Custodian. A drowsy Aaron began to slowly sit up on the lounge; his clothes and hair damp from being out in the rain.

"Are you okay?" Noah queried curiously. From upstairs there suddenly came the slamming sound of a door. Startled, he turned and looked at Perry, "What the hell was that?" Suddenly, a thud-like noise of something falling over upstairs quickly pursued the slamming of the door. "Go."

Swiftly, Perry expanded his magic and used his power of Astral Projection.

~*~

Upstairs, in the attic - filled with the warm golden light - red glittering energy culminated into a human figure and then in a flash, Perry manifested. Glancing about he acknowledged nothing out of the ordinary at eye level. Turning his head and then looking down he observed a figure clad in wet, black clothes kneeling on the floor with its back to him.

"May I help you with something?" he blurted out arrogantly. The figure rose, its long and wet dark hair curled around and over the individual's right shoulder. Realizing who it was, he became less territorial, "Rafaela." She and him exchanged an odd stare, wincing, his power of Premonition was triggered and his eyes were forced shut. Gasping, he reopened them and she was still standing before him. "But I know you," he murmured, not entirely convinced of what he was seeing or saying, "I've fought against you and vanquished your demons."

He began to analyze her features from her torn and ruined gown to her thick, damp, dark hair and then finally, her broken horns. Before he could respond to his observations the attic door suddenly burned with red energy and then exploded into pieces. Lowering her hands; Johdi confidently strode into the room with Noah right behind her. Halting on either side of the Astral Projection of Perry, they too were startled at the presence of their dethroned adversary.

"I've seen the future." Perry blocked them both with his arms, "But I am more curious to know why have you come here? ...of all places."

Calming herself before she replied, Rafaela instantly became uneasy as, an equally as damp, Aaron crept out from behind his brothers and cousin. She turned her head slightly and looked at them with cautious eyes; realizing Noah and Perry were none-the-wiser.

"The mighty Rafaela," Aaron remarked in an egotistic voice, "in the home of the Pogue Witches. The evil bitch that destroyed our family and drove our magic apart... has fate brought you here die?" He made an evil smirk.

"And I suppose," Rafaela spoke with utter arrogance and repulsion toward Aaron, "you've seen your own reflection? It probably speaks better virtue than the bullshit that spills out of your mouth."

Retaliating, Johdi defended Aaron's honor by swaying her hand and firing a bolt of glittering red energy at the Demigoddess. Channeling the unconscious witch behind her on the floor, Rafaela created a barrier of energy with Isadora's power, creating a brilliant flash and harsh explosion when both attacks collided.

Perry's voice moved through her mind, "You're empathic?" A second apparition of him, outside of his brother's and cousin's senses and power, stepped around the dethroned demon, whispering in her ears. "Is this how you reimburse others? You channel someone else and provide their power- "

She turned her head and acknowledged him. "You activated the sundial and I was provided." Rafaela's visage was without horns; instead of her ruined gown she wore the beige rags of someone from an ancient time. "I was molded, long after I was made."

Perry stared at her, stumped, what did she mean?

Promptly, Aaron took Noah's hand. Clapping together with magic, upon Noah taking Perry's hand, his Astral Projection became corporeal and then his hand interlocked with Johdi's. A supernatural groan of something colossal moved about the home and then it suddenly shook. Downstairs, the real Perry, frozen in his position while using his powers, felt immense power surge through every fiber of his body, causing him to inhale sharply and the pupils in both his eyes to dilate dramatically.

"The Pogue Witches," Aaron smirked as he and Rafaela exchanged an intense glare, "are reunited. Are you," the pupils in each of their eyes were dilated to the full size of their eyes and the air around them warped with magic. All their natural instincts became negated as the rich taste of power overwhelmed them, "ready to feel our power, Rafaela?" The windows in the attic spontaneously blew out and a gale force wind moved throughout the room. "The almighty Rafaela, Demigoddess of the Avatarians. Before us, ready to die."

Sensing the intensification of their combined power, Rafaela took the opportunity to retreat. Swaying her arms out like a ballerina, she rapidly spun around on the spot and turned into a black magical mass that swooped about in the air. Touching the floor again right beside Isadora as she lay unconscious on the floor, Rafaela resumed her humanoid form.

"Two can play your game, Aaron Pogue." Extending her arm and aiming her rigidly gestured hand at Perry, she flicked her fingers and commanded in Latin, "Reditum. (Return)"

Quickly, placing her hand upon the young witch, the both of them vanished in a burst of black smoke. Spontaneously, Perry's astral form abruptly disappeared in a flash of red light. Deactivated, the hands of the four witches were released from one another.

Regaining his faculties, Noah was unaware of Isadora's abduction.

~*~

D ownstairs, a magical slingshot occurred. Forcibly slammed back into his body, Perry was thrown backward through the doorway and slammed into the wall out by the front door. Rendered unconscious, as he fell face-first onto the floor and then a few seconds later, the sound of footsteps approached from the right. A pair of black stilettos stopped right beside Perry's head, squatting down, a woman folded her pleated grey skirt underneath her thighs as she reached her arm out and began to caress his dark hair.

"You knew it was only a matter of time." With her free hand, the woman curled her long purple hair back behind her left ear. "I cannot have you spilling Rafaela's dirty little secret and I certainly won't have you trying to foil our plans."

A male's voice stirred behind her, "Asterix."

"You're no fun," the woman now named Asterix complained and then sprinkled glittering fairy dust over Perry's head. "We dark fairies do not take kindly to orders."

An apparition of Asmodeus lingered behind her. "And I could remove you from existence with the snap of my finger. Now do as you're told and enter his nightmares."

Asterix narrowed her eyes and expressed fury, she hated being dictated too. *Dark Fairies are impulsive, arrogant and enslaved fiends that have similar motives to Nightmare Soldiers. They're capable of Dream Manipulation but tend to feed on the life force of humans until the victim, in a final plea, agrees to offer their soul in exchange for freedom. They are skilled at stealing the powers of witches and feeding on their magic. To control this specie of fairy the bargain tends to be great, like the soul of a human or the human they've been assigned to torment. They are invisible to most senses, but are easily detected by witches who can manipulate energy.* The palms of her hands and green eyes shone a brilliant emerald as she used her fairy magic on Perry.

~*~

I n her black smoke form, Rafaela coursed through the air down the middle of City Mall. Veering to the left, her mass raced along King Gustav Boulevard; weaving in and out of the traffic she went by, invisible, as she blended in with the dark. Headed south, she came to the sprawling Logan square; focal point of the Hellmouth beneath the city. Abruptly shooting upwards toward the night sky, she then suddenly plummeted back down toward the square's large water fountain. Secretly, one of many magical gateways down into the Underworld, it gave off a supernatural, amber glow, and Rafaela passed through it as she reentered the gloomy and unfriendly world below.

After the destruction she brought to her elegant lair, Rafaela had taken refuge in another. Perhaps it was not as big, but equally as beautiful as her previous abode... in her opinion. As demons do, occupying caves and grottos, Rafaela's lair was inside a cave in the side of a jagged cliff-face and typical of her, overlooked the ocean. To say she loved a panoramic view would be an understatement, at the very least.

At the opening of the cave, from ceiling to floor were six even spaced Grecian columns. Although filled completely with natural light, Rafaela still felt the need for a colossal sized - the width of two sedans side by side - crystal chandelier that levitated directly in the lairs center. Directly beneath was a long white marble table. Slate covered the floor instead of the usual dirt like the rest of the Underworld.

Spiraling down from the ceiling, causing the chandelier to sway, Rafaela retook her human form in a kneeling position upon her black smoke touching the floor with Isadora lying on the ground before of her. Straightening up, she began to walk away from the captive and unconscious witch, toward the columns that adorned the balcony that looked out over the ocean. Her ruined gown gave off a golden shine and her complete attire became more modern: black stilettos, lace stockings up to her knees, a pair of short black shorts, red satin blouse and a black vest over the top. Her long dark hair was styled in a mess as it hung around both sides of her face and put an emphasis on the stubs that protruded from her forehead where her regal gazelle horns once were.

"Awaken."

Swaying her arm, she gestured her hand in Isadora's direction. Her body gave off a subtle, hot pink glow and she quickly began to stir. Opening her eyes, each of Isadora's indigo colored irises shone a distinct and influential indigo as she began to elevate her head from the floor until she sat upright. Her long, dark, red-infused auburn colored hair was no longer pulled back in a ponytail but instead curled around and over her shoulder.

Isadora's eyes relaxed and she brushed the dirt from her cheek.

"Why am I here?" she growled irritably, staring at Rafaela's back. "You have taken a great deal from the world- "

Turning around, Rafaela hastily approached and elegantly raising her arm out in front of her, she gestured her hand; elevating Isadora from the floor.

"And what about what the world has taken from me?" Their eyes deepened in color. Rafaela showed true anguish. "I did not choose this, this chose me. They took me, molded me, and elevated me into a position of power." With a sway of her hand, she threw Isadora to the side and turned away as she began to rant. "I betrayed them, turned my back on them. They are the Duodecim, great and powerful demons. Insisting I use the power of a Hellmouth to release them from the pocket they are trapped in, in the deepest, depths of the Underworld. But I chose not to. I chose to forge my own path, I rallied an army. What I did not measure was how powerful you Pogue Witches were. You protect this Hellmouth thoroughly, thwart me at every turn. There is nothing secret about betrayal, it is, what it is."

Isadora coughed, brushed herself off and rose back up onto her feet. "Oh god, this isn't going to be an episode of Doctor Phil is it?" She brushed the dirt from her hair. "I kind of have children that I need to tend to."

Swiftly, Rafaela vanished and reappeared behind the young witch. "I really don't care. Desperate times call for desperate measures, you're my leverage," and hastily with the aid of her telekinesis, she moved Isadora in an accelerated blur and then suddenly stopped her again. "Asmodeus is a decent size threat," she acknowledged, almost with great respect for her evil opponent. Snapping her fingers she made flames spontaneously combust atop candles that created a circle around Isadora. "I have waited my entire life to have the power I was entitled to eons ago. Sure, if Asmodeus kills Aaron, Noah and Perry, I get all of it, but at the same time they're entitled to it too."

Confused, and a bit outraged, Isadora turned side-on and attempted to leave the Spirit Prison. Greeted with a flash of light and a mild bang, she was thrown backward onto the ground.

"You see precious, Indigo." Rafaela stood in the middle of the half circle balcony adorned with Grecian columns, "You're a descendant of Fate." *Rafaela envisioned Atropos as a young woman with long blonde hair named Alkina, in a tall grass under golden rays of sunshine frolicking around naked as butterflies moving around her.* "I want you to use your Pogue Magic to summon your first ancestor."

Flicking her hair back, Isadora's fury fueled, and incandescent indigo-colored eyes shone a deep purple. With the aid of her talisman around her neck - her star sign - the symbol of

Capricorn, she was able to harness energy that her body could not provide to use her Sonic Scream ability. At its center the large purple-colored jewel shone. Energy quickly began to wash out over the floor as it emanated from her body. With the elegance of a marionette puppet she used her power of Energy Manipulation to Levitate up and off the floor inside the Spirit Prison.

"Why should I help you?" Isadora growled with a deep voice as her eyes shone with intimidating power. "You have brought nothing but pain to me and my family."

Rafaela stared at the young witch, humbled by the way she expressed her magic. "I admire you Isadora." The two of them exchanged a stare. "You are everything I was supposed to be. Instead I was molded into this, a demon."

"You know nothing about me," Isadora yelled back.

Rafaela smirked. "Oh but I do," she winked. "I knew you as Spectra, goddess of the stars, all those years ago in Ancient Babylon. You were the daughter of planetary deity, Pluto. But this time around, you're Isadora Pogue and your powers are quite befitting to the life you once lived. You're quite expressive in the way you wield your Photokinesis and manipulate energy. Those two boys of yours would make perfect- "

Hearing her antagonist put forward the notion of turning her sons evil, Isadora, took a deep breath and then released a deafening scream. The sheer potency cast out ripples of energy, obliterated the Spirit Prison scattering the candles in various directions. Ceasing her Sonic Scream and swiftly swinging her right arm forward, she blasted Rafaela with light from her hand, throwing the demoness backward into one of the Grecian columns on the balcony causing it to crack.

"You," having moved in the blink of an eye, she appeared at Rafaela and picked her up from the scruff of her top with a glare that almost intimidated the Demigoddess, "touch my sons and you will wish you'd been born a demon rather than molded."

Flicking her hand against Isadora's abdomen, Rafaela threw her backward with a blast of dark photokinetic light. Screaming, she crashed through the table, turning it over and rolled across the floor until she lay still.

"Summon, Atropos." Rafaela approached the witch with a pissed off voice as she watched her get back up onto her feet. "You will summon our first ancestor-"

Turning her head and looking over her shoulder, Isadora spoke, "Why should I?"

"Because," Rafaela seemed to calm herself and show human emotion, "because I need you to summon her so that she can save me."

Isadora turned around and with a curious look on her dirty face she queried, "Why would an ancestor of mine, help a demon like-"

In a flash of light, and burst of golden energy, Atropos, Alkina - one of the three Original Witches - appeared in Rafaela's lair. Her long, golden blonde hair floated around both sides of her face and she wore a short, Grecian gown.

DESCEND INTO DARKNESS

"Have the textbooks of scholars lead you astray, Rafaela?"

Her demeanor was rather forward and belittling, confident and egotistical. "Fate is absolute. My sisters and I are everywhere. You don't need her blood to summon me. Just speak my name; I can hear it resonate throughout the multiverse as though I am standing right beside you. I knew you once." Their stern eyes drawn to one another like magnets. "Once, when you were the beautiful girl I had named, Saturn."

In the background, Isadora's fury fueled, glowing purple eyes softened, and the bejeweled talisman of Capricorn around her neck lost its shine as its power returned to slumber. The colossal chandelier brought out the blood-red in her auburn colored hair.

"This seems to become more and more absurd," she grumbled aloud. Atropos glanced over her shoulder and observed the witch. "A deity is siding," Isadora spat with repulsion, "with a fricken de–" With little effort and the snap of her fingers, Atropos rendered the witch unconscious on the ground.

Swiftly, Atropos glanced at Rafaela out of the corner of her eye; "Lucky you can pick your friends, better than you can pick your family." The dethroned evil leader raised an eyebrow in caution. "I can alter your form, hide this," she waved her hand about feverishly at Rafaela, "horrid visage you wear so casually."

Taken aback Rafaela spoke, "You'd help me?"

"Long before there was anything, I was a witch," Atropos began to tell the story of her origin and possibly others, "beautiful as I am powerful. My sisters and I, the Venefica, as the Divinita referred to us, worshipped the Universalis Solarium. It was the source of our divine power." Rafaela stood silent, unintentionally captivated by the story. "Mortals ought to forget the stories woven by the mouths of men about witches, because being a witch is not to worship dark entities such as Lucifer. Every good witch on earth receives their powers from a celestial source."

Rafaela realized. "The Universalis Solarium."

"Every witch born on earth is a descendant of me and my sisters." Atropos traced her fingertips across the overturned table as she walked along it. "Before our death at the hands of our sister, Malus, our descendants spread about the world along with our counterparts, the Romani-"

"Wretched fiends," Rafaela growled irritably.

Atropos shot her a dagger-filled glare. "You ought to play nice, Rafaela. The power of those fiends has stopped every single demon and evil witch you've sent after them. Alera obviously did not teach you how to weigh up your opponent." The godly blonde woman eyed the demoness up and down with chauvinistic eyes. "But then again, she wasn't your mother to begin with, she only altered your perception into thinking she was."

Retaliating at the few home truths, Rafaela screamed and released a blast of dark photokinetic light from her hands only to have the deity catch it in her hand, clench it and reduce it to dust.

"I am beyond your power, child. Perhaps this is why the Disciples employed Asmodeus to overthrow your position in the hierarchy of the Underworld. You've become comfortable with all this reimbursing crap you've been trying to achieve." Atropos made a smirk that mocked the beautiful, broken horn demoness. "Only a bigot tries to persuade the masses into believing one's own idiot idealism." She gave Rafaela a curious look and questioned her sarcastically, "You're not an idiot, are you, Rafaela?"

Rafaela narrowed her glare.

"From me," Atropos moved away from the overturned table and continued to tell her story, "The Pogue Line of Witches began. You're a destiny bound bloodline. It became the destiny of the line to protect the most powerful Hellmouth–"

Rafaela uttered, "Treadwell."

Atropos glanced at the demoness. "It was Babylon long before it was Treadwell, my dear. Your comrade Callidora turned against you and banished you from this dimension. But long before that, I would watch you play as children. You were the children of Lindsay Hogue, a descendant of mine."

Gasping, Rafaela felt a searing pain in her head. *Closing her eyes, Atropos forced the demoness to see her earliest memory as a child, with golden locks playing with three brothers in the yard of a mud-brick home in Jerusalem.*

"Alera murdered the boys." Atropos moved her rigid hand, releasing the demoness from her power. "Took you as her own and Lindsay was none-the-wiser. Protecting their souls, I had Maria turn them into the deities Pluto, Mars and Venus. I was able to recapture your soul when Alera had you sell it as a young girl. I crafted it into Saturn."

"I need you to save me." Rafaela stumbled through a pit of emotion. "Asmodeus will kill me." Atropos simply stared, curious, as she observed the mercy-begging-expression on the demon's face. "Killing me changes the fate of everyone. Why do you think I took the witch. She is my leverage against them. They won't risk any harm coming to precious Isadora. But I guess even fate is blind-sided by ego and power... "

Insulted, Atropos shoved her arm out in front and flicked her fingers at Rafaela, blasting her with energy. Thrown backward, the demigoddess slammed into a Grecian column and remained pinned against it, forced to watch her fate approach. Using her unholy, demigoddess power, Rafaela appeared to effortlessly pull away from the column.

"And here I thought," she retorted sarcastically, leaning her neck left and then right as she prepared for a fight, "we were related." Flicking her fingers as she swayed her arms out, Rafaela blasted the fate with heated energy. "I guess not, Atropos."

Struck by Rafaela's Molecular Combustion power, the deity of fate was catapulted backward into the overturned table. Leaving the balcony area of her new lair, the dethroned leader glided cross the floor as she attempted to strike again.

"Hand of fate." Atropos, invisible, suddenly appeared behind Rafaela. With a brisk gesture of her hand, she made it glow gold and wove a new fate for the demoness. "You're a demon. Do you think I can be fooled? You possess no humanity. Posing as their sister from another life would enable you to physically steal their magic for your own selfish need to re-dominate the Underworld, vanquish them and Asmodeus."

Rafaela taunted the fate-less room, "It appears fate has escaped me."

"Well played," Asmodeus smirked, "Rafaela."

An uneasy Rafaela replied, "Surmising will make an ass of you, Asmodeus."

"Trying to trick the Fate into curing you of your evil?" They exchanged a certain stare that revealed they both knew the hidden agenda. "Let's face it, we both know you're pure demon and the girl you once were all those years ago, in Babylon, is long dead. The day you relinquished you're soul as Saturah, you lost your ties to the Pogue Family Tree and any magic it would pass down to future descendants."

"I tried to find the new host of my soul," Rafaela revealed sarcastically, "Atropos the spiteful bitch hid it well."

"Fate belongs to everyone: not just good, you dim-witted woman. No one is above it. But you seem to forget the minor detail," Asmodeus said and walked out from behind the overturned table, "I am in charge of your fate." Rafaela stiffened her posture as she watched him walk out from behind the obstruction. Atropos had changed her fate. "I do not care for the Pogue Witches, they are nothing compared to what I can do to you." Trembling, tears escape the corner of Rafaela's eyes as she felt her heart race unbearably in her chest. "You've had your time; you've had your power. Now," he paused, the light streamlined his slim suit and physique, "it's time to leave the fate of evil in capable hands. It's my turn."

Rafaela let out a scream as her body was ravished by flames, from her feet to her abdomen. Arching her back she clenched her eyes tightly and then finally exploded into a flurry of flames. Meeting her demise at the hands of Asmodeus, Rafaela was vanquished.

"So yes," he smirked egotistically, proud of his achievement as he addressed the pile of ash before him, "I can save you."

Turning around, he observed Isadora for a moment, smiling at her beauty. He brushed his hand past his mouth as he pondered the endless possibilities of turning her evil. Placing his other hand in his suit, pants pocket, he began to approach her with a smug swagger. He was sly, incapable of loyalty to his own brethren but possessed enough proficiency to elevate evil to a new level in the world.

"You are quite," he stopped before the unconscious Isadora, "the specimen." He slowly began to kneel down to examine her a little closer. "Such beauty–"

Reaching out to touch her auburn hair, a flash of purple energy protected her, singed his fingers and repulsion of the powerful magic forced him to stagger backward. Standing upright, he at first glared down at her but then quickly took a half step back again as he observed a figure slip out of the dark. A very masculine and naked male with long golden locks and ram horns on his head lowered his arm to his side.

"The witch is protected by me," it spoke in a deep, intimidating voice.

Asmodeus continued to observe and then spoke curiously, "A zodiac."

It spoke proud, "I am Capricorn."

Asmodeus was uncertain if he could contend with the power of a zodiac and was all but about to flee when he turned and bumped into Connemara Penthal. Her long, auburn hair with a blood-red tone, everybody always said Isadora had her mother's hair, thick with volume hung down both sides of her narrow face. Her green eyes intimidated Asmodeus as she simply stared at him. Her glossed red lips were crumpled with bitterness, like a territorial mother confronting her child's bully.

He smirked, sensing a familiarity. "Ah, Callidora."

"Don't touch my daughter." And with a brisk gesture of her hands, flicking her fingers, she used the power of Molecular Combustion on Asmodeus to blast him into scattering molecules. "When will people learn," she growled nastily. Hurrying over to her daughter as she lay on the ground, Connemara roused Isadora, making her come too. "Indy."

For a moment incoherent, Isadora murmured, "Mom."

"Isadora, I don't have long." Connemara hurried her daughter up onto her feet. "You need to know that I love you. But we don't have much time. My magic is failing." Her voice frantic and hopeful that her daughter would empathize.

"What do you mean? You're magic is failing?" Isadora spat with confusion.

"I placed Illusions around our family. Everything about the Pogue Family is an Illusion. I've done things I am not proud of and now those–"

Letting out a scream, Isadora grabbed at the side of her head as immense pain tore through her mind. Mortified, Connemara tried to confront her daughter only to be repelled backward by black and grey energy. Noticing it, she became cautious; almost convinced that Asmodeus' evil had gotten to her daughter. Letting out a sudden shriek, the body of the powerful illusionist witch abruptly left in a flash of red astral energy and harshly recoiled back into her body as she stood before a full length mirror in the Siren Sorority Compound.

~*~

Across the county border in Hoxton County, the moonlight captured the busy Circular Quay of Sandhurst. The modern financial sector of the monolithic city, vastly greater than Treadwell a county over, was imposing on the green and mustard-yellow ferries as they came into dock. To the left side of the water-transport hub was a massive cruise liner. A further hundred feet into the financial district, in Hayden Park, stood a presidential, white-house inspired building with the Greek symbols Ωω for Omega across the front above the main entry. The street view visage swayed like water and then morphed into skyscrapers and hotels. This was how the Sorority hid themselves from mortal eyes and their predators but mostly, Sabar the Sabarticar Demon.

In the main sitting area of the Siren Sorority Compound, the same place Asmodeus had pretended to be Maria, Queen of Good Magic to retrieve information, Connemara was repelled from the mirror and crashed onto the polished floorboards, skidding a short distance before stopping against the wall on the opposite side of the room.

"Oh," she remarked in a bewildered state, "what the hell was that?"

Casually stepping out from behind a marble column, Aaron Pogue revealed himself. "Hello Connor. Fancy seeing you here. It's a bit rich for someone of your poor taste, don't you think?"

Getting up onto her feet, Connemara curiously observed her brother-in-law. She closed her eyes, inhaled deeply and then reopened them. For a moment they glowed purple as she used her powers to sense, and then the glow faded as she made the acknowledgment, "I am amazed how you of all people got past security." They both exchanged a look of familiarity. "Who are you trying to kid, Ravenna? I smell your true form. Posing as Aaron would only fool an idiot."

He retorted sarcastically, giving himself away, "I got past the Sirens did I not?"

"You're the one who put my astral form back in my body," Connemara stated the obvious. "You've put Isadora in grave danger, leaving her alone in the Underworld. I–"

Aaron resumed Ravenna's female form, "I have no particular interest, witch. I only care for the moment that Asmodeus kills the Pogue Witches and we use their power to release the Twelve Disciples from their prison." Smirking she waved her hand past her face and magically resumed the visage of Aaron Pogue as Connemara looked on with disgust. "As long as we are here, let's make it our goal to get along." He grinned at her eagerly. "Or your daughter dies."

Concealed behind a column, the real Connemara hid with fear written across her face having used her power of Illusory to create a clone of herself and the mirror to send an Astral Projection to Isadora.

"I won't let another daughter die," she huffed, and as she turned away she magically vanished in glittering light. Reappearing in another room in glittering light, Connemara strode to the center, waved her hand and lowered another illusion to reveal a Spirit Prison. "Imitation is the greatest form of flattery." Snapping her fingers, the flames ignited atop the candles that created the Spirit Prison and then with another snap, she created a second clone of herself. "Keep up pretenses, pet. Mummy dearest has some work to do."

In glittering light the real Connemara teleported out of the S.S Compound.

~*~

Venturing down the staircase that curved with the circular room of the house, Noah and Aaron bickered - the usual occurrence when they were ever together - as Johdi walked between them.

"I expect you to know what the hell that was, Aaron." Noah growled with frustration as he waved his arm and hand in flurry. "It only happened when you touched my hand."

Aaron protested, "How do I know? I gave up my magic, remember. I am technically a mortal again. In case your pigheaded brain forgot that part, Noah."

Johdi grumbled beneath her breath, "Fight you bastards, I hate peace."

Abruptly, Noah stopped on the staircase, Johdi swayed sideways up against the wall as Noah reached his arm forward and pointed at Aaron. "YOU," he yelled, releasing his anger, "YOU, come into my house and preach about being mortal. It was your decision. You're the gutless one. You ran like a coward from your magic, from being a witch."

Aaron, smug and thirsty to break his young brother's neck stepped down and brushed Noah's arm to the side, "You really want to have this fight?" His amber colored eyes were stern and almost revealed the evil that secretly hid behind them. Noah's blue sapphire eyes deepened. "Good old, Noah. Custodian to all of those in Treadwell. How courageous–" Out of nowhere, Noah punched him in the face, turned and continued down the staircase.

A speechless Johdi stood to the side. Suddenly, she spoke, "Whatever it was it was evil. I could feel it, feel it, trying to possess me."

Aaron acted oblivious, feeling victimized.

Venturing on down the stairs, Noah halted at the bottom as he turned his head to the left and noticed Perry lying on the floor. Quickly, he fell to his knees at his brother's side.

Perry." Holding his hands over his brother's head, Noah tried to heal his brother of his unknown ailment. "Come on, Perry," he growled beneath his breath, "wake up."

Quickly, Johdi and Aaron came down the stairs.

Opening his eyes, Perry reached forward as he gasped for air.

Chapter Fourteen

BETTER THE DEVIL YOU KNOW

Noah Pogue was different. The lighting was gloomy and low instead of golden and warm. Sitting upright on the floor, Perry expanded his chest as he inhaled and then sighed as he regained his faculties. Everything appeared normal to him... well as normal, as normal could be. Turning his head to his left he observed the front double doors, glancing ahead he looked into a shadow-filled lounge room and then turning his head to the right, a gloomy circular foyer and dark stairs that lead up into an abyss of black.

"Noah?" he called out but received only silence, "Johdi?" Getting to his feet, the weak light accentuated his tall and slender figure. Perry wore skinny denim jeans and a charcoal button-up shirt with the sleeves folded up to his elbows. "Aaron," the name tasted like acid as he reluctantly spoke the name. "Hello?"

Behind him, invisible to his senses, a woman with long dark purple hair lingered in his silhouette. Her eyes shone a luminescent emerald as she manipulated him with her dark fairy magic. Waving her hands about his head, streams of apple green energy filtered in through his ears and enriched his own green eyes.

"Dreams of a world, sown so well, I bid you Perry show me your hell," she whispered a simple spell in his ear.

"Perry," a child's voice summoned from another part of the house. "Perry." Adult Perry Pogue stiffened his posture, knowing the voice of the child was his as the boy about ten years old ran off the *staircase and skidded to a stop in the middle of the circular foyer. "Are you coming or not?"*

He stuttered, "What?" Emotion welling up in his eyes. "Who–?" He clenched his fists as they hung either side of his body. "I don't want to go," he murmured, his voice stricken with fear. "Please wake up, please wake up," he closed his eyes and repeated to himself. "Come on Perry," reopening his eyes, he was still in the gloomy surroundings, "wake up."

~*~

Kneeling on the floor beside Perry, Noah's attention was solely

focused on trying to wake his brother. Oblivious to the floor above while their attention too was placed on Perry. Johdi and Aaron's witch and mortal senses failed to sense the presence of a brunette woman clad in green satin fabric as she walked the length of the banister above them before disappearing. Stepping out of Aaron's shadow, she reappeared and like Asterix was a fairy as displayed by her unique hot pink eyes, but on the side of good. Her long, brunette hair fell down both sides of her long and narrow face. On closer observation, she was dressed in a multi-green colored, satin, Indian Sari with a delicate and decorative silver chain in her hair with a large jewel that sat in the center of her forehead.

~*~

"Come along." *The child beamed an innocent smile at adult*

Perry from the middle of the gloomy foye., "Come along, Perry." Magically, his figure rose and shapeshifted into a woman with long blood-red hair and indigo colored eyes. "Come sweet boy, it's time for bed."

His voice fled between his parted lips, "Mom." As he acknowledged the woman before him with a look of intimidation. "This is a dream. I know this is. You're dead." Suddenly, against his will, he began to amble forward toward his mother. "Please." Swiftly the house turned into his childhood home and memories quickly came flooding back, "Please, don't make me do it. I don't want to do this anymore."

Turning suddenly as he regained control for a split second, his green eyes peered into the glowing eyes of the purple haired fairy whose magic was bewitching him. Looking her over he was able to get a quick description and was then turned around against his own will.

"Don't be silly," Lindsay Pogue's soft hand took his hand and the two began to walk toward a bedroom door labeled 'Perry', "I am not dead. But you'll be toast if your father finds out that you're not in bed."

Perry dug his heels into the floor, but his mother's strength was impressive as he slid across the floorboards. She turned the door handle on his bedroom door, pushed it open and a dimly-lit room with a bay-window unfolded before him. Lindsay entered the room, crossing the threshold, Perry expecting to enter against his will was suddenly stopped by an invisible barrier that flashed gold for a second before disappearing into the doorframe.

"Oh thank god," he sighed with relief.

Standing behind, Asterix narrowed her eyes viciously. "You cannot refuse my dark fairy magic, Perry Pogue."

From the further area of the hallway, came a sudden burst of golden light. Shrieking, Asterix raised her arms and hands to her face to shield herself. Gesturing with her hands, dark-purple energy ignited as her dark magic took a full, front on assault of good fairy *magic. Some distance away, the woman who had haunted Noah's home moments earlier, now manifested herself in this reality.*

"You always were a sly fiend, any wonder our Fairy Republic is in such disarray, Asterix. And now I understand why," said the brunette woman dressed in her multi-green colored Indian Sari. "The only thing you will achieve by torturing a Pogue Witch is a slow and painful vanquish."

Briskly flicking her fingers, there came off a burst of dark-purple energy, Asterix froze time and engaged her good opponent.

"Oh, Alessia," she sighed sarcastically. "You can have your republic. I am aligned with Asmodeus. With his potency we will bring about a darker period far greater than the miniscule attempt Rafaela executed. The Hellmouth will open under his influence and hell will be unleashed, starting with Treadwell and then the entire globe."

Alessia's aura glittered with gold energy. "You're an idiot, girl. We're benevolent beings; we do not execute acts of evil. I cannot allow you to harm the witch." She swayed her hand out and conjured glittering, golden energy within her grasp.

Swiftly, extending her arm forward, Asterix projected a blast of purple energy at Alessia. Struck, the good fairy shrieked and was banished in a flash of golden light. Swaying her hands at Perry's back, Asterix resumed control over him.

"Enter."

~*~

In the foyer of Noah's house, Aaron silently observed his brothers on the floor. Glancing across into the lounge room, the glow of Pridham's amethyst colored Custodian eyes caught his attention. Failing to remember that she was still in the house, he promptly extended his arm and then gestured his hand at her. Silently using her magic, although to his family Aaron had relinquished his powers, Rasima trapped Pridham within the room, and with another wave of his hand, he made her invisible and muted her voice.

Raising his finger to his lip, Aaron mouthed 'shh' at her.

Between Noah, Perry and the front door a sudden burst of bright, grainy and glowing, golden energy began to manifest. In an abrupt flash of green, Alessia revealed herself. With a swing of her arm, she tore Noah away from his brother and sent him soaring backward into the lounge room. Landing on the table, it broke apart under the weight of his body.

"Noah," Pridham shrieked fearfully.

Having hidden to the side of the doorway as the Pogue Witch soared through it, Pridham quickly ran to her comrade's aid. Kneeling down on the floor beside him, she began to heal him. A light began to shine out of her hands as she placed one at the side of his head and the other on the exposed skin of his abdomen where his clothes had folded upwards.

~*~

Powerful and deeply attractive, Alessia, stepped forward as she glared at Aaron Pogue but completely dismissing Johdi Fox. Swaying her hand she conjured a ball of grainy, golden glowing energy and then with a rapid swing of her arm she threw her magical attack at the Pogue brother. Striking him in the torso, he cried out and was thrown backward, slamming into the wall before falling face first onto the floor.

"Who are you?" Johdi spat, her aura igniting with vibrant, red energy. Extending her arm, energy gathered into her rigidly gestured hand as she prepared to fire a magical attack of her own. "What do you want?"

Swiftly, in-between the milliseconds that it took to blink, Alessia disappeared and then reappeared directly in front of Johdi. Waving her hand at the witch, the fairy was able to suppress the red energy back inside her body.

"I am a good fairy of the fairy republic." Her hot pink eyes were highly attractive in which to gaze. "My name is Alessia. You are Johdi Fox, the witch of fear who can turn a mortal to stone if I am correct?"

The two women exchanged a stare of knowing.

"Why did you attack Noah?" Johdi queried, her tone quickly becoming guarded. "What did he do wrong to you," she spat sarcastically, "fairy?"

Alessia stared at the witch, silently observing every fiber of her being. Spontaneously, her eyes shone a delightful lilac and then returned to their original hot pink.

"You're not the demon," she explained.

Insulted, Johdi felt the urge to blow up the seductive creature before her. "I should bloody think so. How dare you call me a demon. Tell me why I shouldn't crush you with your fears?"

Alessia showed her harmonious smile. "Girl, we fairies are significantly more powerful than witches. It is you who should be scared of what I could do to you."

"And here I thought you were a benevolent race," Johdi spat sarcastically.

Alessia retorted, "Same goes to you, witch. We're in shadowy times. Rafaela's tyranny split the entire magical community in half. She came within inches of resurrecting Alera and corrupting the Hellmouth beneath Treadwell. You and Isadora prevented that by vanquishing the nightmare soldier, Kamenwati. As far as great evils throughout history goes, she is near the top.

She was, is, the Whore of Babylon. She would spare the lives of good magical creatures and witches if they sided with evil. Their reward would be that she would reimburse them with power."

An intelligent Johdi picked up on one word, "What do you mean, was?"

"Oh," Alessia smirked knowingly, "you didn't know?" glancing out the corner of her eye; she caught a glimpse of Aaron starting to get up from the floor. Focusing back on the witch in front of her, she spoke with stern eyes, "Rafaela has been vanquished. Asmodeus has taken her throne and planted a demon inside the circle of Pogue Witches. It could be any one of them." Elevating her hand to her mouth, she took a deep breath and blew fairy dust in Johdi's face.

Staggering backward, Johdi coughed and fanned the glittering dust away from her and when she went to retaliate she acknowledged that the fairy was gone. Staggering on his feet for a moment, Aaron brushed his blond hair from his face and then flicked his eyes up, hoping for the fairy to still be in the house so he could unleash retribution upon her.

"I forgot how powerful fairies are." To the side, standing on the staircase, he saw Johdi rubbing her eyes. "But how quickly they forget how powerful I am." He straightened himself up and then growled beneath his breath as he began to approach his cousin, "I am Rasima Straig." Keeping up pretences, Aaron stopped at the foot of the stairs and queried Johdi, "Are you okay, Johdi?"

A vague Johdi murmured, "Hmm... yeah, I'm fine." Flashing in her mind, she recounted the fairy Alessia blowing something in her face, "The bitch blew dust in my face."

"We need to get upstairs to the book," Aaron reached his arm forward and touched her on the forearm, "so we can find out who we're up against."

Upon his sinister touch, her magic reacted and she was overcome by darkness again, displayed through the dilation of the pupils in her eyes for a brief moment.

"Sure," she replied, her voice deepened by the toxic touch, "I agree. Let's consult the Book of Shadows." Turning and venturing upstairs, Johdi under Aaron's evil influence dismissed Perry as he lay on the floor and an absent Noah who vanished after being thrown into the lounge room by Alessia.

Pausing for a moment on the bottom step, Aaron watched his cousin disappear out of sight as she reached the banister of the second floor. Turning his head, his appearance shrunk and his aura shone as he shapeshifted into Rasima. Her long, thick dark hair fell down her back and over her right shoulder, her bewitching apple-green eyes were brought out by purple eye-shadow and mascara. A purple shawl draped over her shoulders and curled over both her forearms, skin-tight leather pants and a burgundy corset accentuated her breasts. Rasima stared at Perry, smiling at how easy it had been for a fairy to subdue and render him comatose and catapult Noah into a pocket prison she had formed in the lounge room.

"I didn't even have to break a sweat," she toyed egotistically. Behind her she felt the presence of another, the shadow of a man dressed in a suit manifested as the air rippled. "My lord," she acknowledged respectfully, turning around she engaged her superior with a bright smile, "Asmodeus. They have not suspected a thing. I managed to touch them, including the cousin and connect their dormant magic to me. All I will have to do is touch the book and we will have what we need to harness the power of the sundial."

Invisible to senses of both the shadow of Asmodeus and Rasima, Alessia reappeared in a burst of grainy, golden energy at the top of the staircase as she watched the two evil beings below. Turning her head, she glanced to the few steps that lead up to the attic and the half-open attic door as Johdi walked about the room. Her resting hands slipped off of the timber banister as she stepped away and then vanished abruptly as she accelerated toward the location of the Pogue relative, leaving a trail of, invisible to the naked eye, golden energy in her wake.

In another burst of grainy, golden energy as she stopped in the middle of the room, Alessia observed Johdi as she fussed about a medium-size table littered with shallow bowls of potion ingredients, slender white flame lit candles and a bubbling cauldron in the middle.

"Johdi," she commanded, her hot pink eyes gave off a glow for a second. "You have become the victim of tactile hypnosis. You need to–" she cut her words short abruptly as she felt her superior's hand rest upon her left shoulder. "My, my, queen."

Moving out of the fairies shadow, Queen Maria of Good Magic and ultimately powerful Old One, dressed in a gown of white with gold embroidery. Her long, brunette hair fell down her back with a delicate crown of gold neatly placed at the forefront as it held the front section of her hair back.

"It's as I feared," Maria's voice held a seductive and heavenly echo. "Darkness has reached their circle. I thought the threat was gone with Rafaela's vanquish, but this threat has been in motion for some time." She turned and faced Alessia. "My child. It is against the laws that I am bound to that keep me from meddling with fate. But this evil will end them all. I need you to break this hypnosis. Free Johdi–" sensing Atropos's infinite power, Maria stopped talking glanced up and then returned her attention on Alessia. "Help the witches." And swiftly she was gone in a burst of white light.

Silent in her agreement, Alessia took a deep breath, turned her head and stared at the witch before moving forward toward her. Approaching from the side, the fairy stopped, raised her hand and then swayed her fingers. Golden energy emerged from

Alessia's fingertips and promptly entered Johdi's eyes and ears. Glittering gold filtered into her eyes as the evil influence broke, her body quivered for a moment and then she was free.

"Go to the book," Alessia whispered into the witch's ear. Turning her head as she rested her hands on the table, Johdi observed the thick, tree-green leather bound book across the room. "You will find the demon you seek, Johdi Fox." In a swift blur of glittering gold energy, Alessia whisked around to the other side of the witch and paused. "Show those who wish you harm who possesses true power."

Leaving the table littered with potion ingredients and a bubbling cauldron behind her, Johdi walked across the warm and well-lit room of golden light; stopping at the book. She placed her hands upon its green, leather cover with a bold octagon symbol with an overlapping pentagram in the middle. Sensing her good magic, the book gave a gold glow. Elevating her face, Johdi looked across at the half-open attic door before returning her gaze downwards at the book and then proceeded to open it.

"I ask of thee, find for me, the demon that haunts inside this house where I reside."

Chapter Fifteen

BETTER THE DEVIL YOU KNOW – PART TWO

Running across Rafaela's lair, Isadora took a deep breath as she went to leap over the stone banister between the Grecian columns.

Beyond was the untrustworthy ocean, realm of ocean god-king Neptune and his wife Salacia who had turned evil under Rafaela's influence. Below the balcony, at the foot of the cliff face was a golden sandy beach which was slapped by crashing waves.

It appeared as a normal cliff face where different shades and layers of brown in the earth were the result of tidal erosion, showing how deep the ocean had been once upon a time. Topping the cliff was a wondrous and never ending forest of native Canadian evergreen trees. Mystic Beach, British Columbia, Canada was located on the southwest side of Vancouver Island and only accessible via the Juan de Fuca Marine Trail.

Out in the water, captured in the panoramic view of Juan de Fuca Strait, a tall ship that was both grandiose in its appearance and presence. Its sails were open but no wind moved them. At a closer glance, the name of the ship was displayed, The Nautica. Although not common knowledge amongst witches or the supernatural community at large, the ship was governed by notorious pirate, Haarlem. When not occupying waters in the human world, it docks at Pirate Cove in the Dream/Spirit Realm.

Leaping over the edge of the balcony, Isadora screamed as invisible and powerful magics reacted to hers. There came a flash and explosion of energy. Thrown backward across the lair, she crashed onto the floor and skidded to a stop.

She groaned as she sat up. With a puff of her breath she blew her hair from her face.

"This is getting old," she growled irritably to herself as she got up onto her feet and brushed herself off. "That darf bitch brought me here, got vanquished and now I'm fricken trapped here."

A sudden chuckle broke the silence. Gasping, Isadora promptly turned around and saw a female warrior clad in Roman gladiator attire with her long blonde hair pulled back.

"We need to stop meeting like this," said the woman, her immortal eyes drew Isadora's to her own like magnets, "Isadora Pogue."

A confused Isadora murmured with caution, "And you are?"

"Diana," the woman stated proudly, "Goddess of the hunt."

Realization struck Isadora when she remembered, "You were in the Dream Realm. Are we in the Underworld?"

"We are far from the Underworld, child." Diana stepped out from behind the overturned table, humble as the witch read the magical energy she gave off. "This is Canada. That's a bit vague, because the country is rugged and vast. I intercepted Rafaela the moment she fled your father's house with you and teleported you both here."

"Err... okay... " Isadora spoke vaguely. "Well if we're not in the Underworld. Which part of Canada are we in then? Pray tell."

"Mystic Beach," Diana revealed, "on Vancouver Island."

Isadora's eyes widened, remembering too well what happened last time she was here. "Oooh... Julyanne is going to be so super-mega pissed off."

Diana replied with half a smirk, "Quite the opposite actually. We've felt the darkness in Treadwell all the way over here. There is a great threat within the confines of your home and Julyanne has taken the liberty to keep you here for your own safety."

Isadora gasped as emotion rose in her eyes, "For my own safety. Rafaela was murdered by another demon. And you're a fricken deity, how could–"

Diana raised her hand, "That was Atropos's doing. Fate is not mine to control."

"I want my children," Isadora became agitated, her motherly instincts began to burn wildly inside of her heart. "Release me. You don't understand; if there is a threat inside my house, I need to protect my sons."

Diana shook her head implying no.

"I SAID LET ME GO!"

Accidentally utilizing her sonic scream power hasty and violent ripples of energy raced at the deity. Struck, although immune to the power, Diana departed in a flash of golden energy.

~*~

*I*nside the Dream Realm, the sound of chirping birds and noises of the forest made Holland Creek Trail near the township of Ladysmith, even more enchanting. Carefully, Shane Penthal stepped through the tempered forest with runners on his feet, sports tank-top and shorts. Taking a moment to catch his breath, he ran his hand through sweaty blond locks and took in his surroundings with his striking blue sapphire eyes.

"I swear this was the way–" he spat irritably.

A female's voice took him by surprise, "To the Haus of Romani?" He cried out in fear and nearly fell over a fallen tree trunk.

The woman simply beamed a radiant smile, "You're a witch." The intrigue glimmered in her eyes.

Staggering to find solid ground, Shane pointed his finger at her with a startled expression. "You scared the shit out of me. Where the hell did you come from?"

She chuckled to herself and then spoke in alluring french, "I come from here and I come from there... " and to his surprise, he understood her perfectly. Then she spoke in english, "I am Daniela, a Woodland Fairy of the Republic."

Her long, two-tone golden and white-blonde hair was styled in a plait that curved around and over her shoulder with leaves and twigs woven throughout. She wore a short moss-green dress with a brown belt and roman sandals. Her hot-pink eyes glimmered as her aura shone with gentle sunlight.

"You-you're a fairy?" he queried suspiciously,

She looked at him with confusion, "You've never met one?" Glancing out the corner of her eye she was able to sense other magic within close proximity. "This journey of yours to the Haus of Romani is one for a later date."

Through the forest, fast moving, green energy approached. In another burst of grainy, green energy a second fairy manifested. This one was Chinese in appearance, long, black hair that fell in curls with delicate twigs woven into it and complimented with a few maple leaves. She was another Woodland Fairy.

"They are coming," she expressed with concern, "they've sensed his location."

Shane queried, "Whose or what are they?" Looking at both fairies.

"They are, Nightmare Soldiers." Daniela's voice trembled. "Now that Rafaela has been vanquished, there is a new evil that plans to attack your family." Startled, the fairies shrieked as bolts of black lightning impaled the tree to the side. "Time to go."

Snatching Shane by the forearm, the three of them teleported out of the Dream Realm in a burst of grainy, gold energy.

Bursts of black smoke rose up from the ground as three pissed off women clad in black manifested.

~*~

I n the attic, lit by the warm, golden glow of the down-lights, Johdi had cast her spell upon it to help identify the demon that was within the house. A supernatural wind repelled her hands away from the cover, flipping it and fluttering the pages until it fell open on a page titled in Latin: *Miles Somnum*... which loosely translated to Nightmare Soldier.

"Oh you've got to be kidding me," she growled beneath her breath,

Aaron spoke, "I was just about to say the same thing." Startling the young woman and not offering an apology. "I thought I was kidding myself, but then it all started to make sense."

Confused, Johdi observed him as he left the door open behind him. "You've lost me, Aaron. I have no idea what you're talking about?"

He paused, smug in body language he folded his arms and despised her, "You. Cousin. I have figured out why you are here. Why you have been hanging around like a bad smell." Johdi was a hard person to insult as she listened with a blank expression on her face. "Your objective is to take my position in the Pogue Family and take my power."

Johdi scoffed at the theory. "You're an idiot. Has anyone ever told you that?" Striking a nerve, Aaron grew silently furious at her lack of respect toward him. "Why on earth would I want to take your position in the family and steal your power? I HAVE MY FRICKEN OWN, THANKS."

Narrowing his eyes, he replied bitterly, "You touch the book. The book honors your presence as though it is your ancestor's blood spilled on the pages across the ages of its existence." Johdi raised an eyebrow as she silently speculated that maybe he was jealous of the idea of a close family, considering he had given everything away and abandoned his family to live out a mortal life. "Perhaps, I ought to touch the book. See if it acknowledges me even though I am mortal now."

Lying on the lounge room floor amongst the rubble of his destroyed coffee table, Noah began to come to and Pridham removed her hands, deactivating the glow of her healing power.

"I thought I had lost you," Pridham, showed him a tenderness that not too many people got to see. "That fairy did a real number on you, Noah."

He coughed. "Fairy? What fairy?" Confused. He never saw Alessia appear to him by the front door as he tended to Perry, so it made sense that he had no recollection of the fairy throwing him with her power of telekinesis. "Pridham, what-what are you doing here? I thought you had left."

Hesitant, she remained silent.

"What is it?" He was quick to sense her discomfort before noticing the look in her eyes. "Pridham, what is it you're not telling me?"

She caved, "Aaron used magic to trap me in here. This room is a prison. I tried to warn you when you were kneeling beside Perry. But he, Aaron, muted my voice; made it so that no one could hear or see me."

Noah looked at her like she was delusional. He knew his brother possessed no magic, he'd seen him relinquish it years ago. "Don't be absurd, Pridham, he relinquished his magic–" He went silent. In his mind he saw himself, an Astral Projection of Perry, Aaron and his cousin Johdi in the attic when Rafaela visited... he remembered Aaron taking him against his will and suddenly becoming overwhelmed by evil to the point that it blocked out all his nature, his good instincts. Glancing back at Pridham, they both exchanged a certain look of panic, "Why didn't I sense it?"

She replied, "Aryan brought me. She insisted I do not allow the three of you touch one another. In your defense, how were you to know though? You thought he was your brother. Aaron... a human. Like any other person would have thought."

Turning his head, he observed Perry still lying on the floor, "Where is Aaron now?"

"Upstairs," she revealed. Turning his head, Noah looked at his fellow Custodian, "He is with Johdi."

Noah became alarmed, "If he touches the book he will regain a portion of his power back since he touched and channeled, myself, Perry and Johdi."

Outside, in the dark, came the sound of a murder, a flock of crows in the front yard as they flew directly at the house. Making impact with the front door, they exploded showering Perry's unconscious body on the other side and the front porch with glass and debris as squawking crows filled the ground level. A figure with a golden aura strode confidently out of the black and through the doorway. The glass and debris crunched beneath Connemara Penthal's boots. She stopped in the middle of the entry way, directly in line with the doorway into the lounge room. Turning her head, although he was invisible to her, Connemara and Noah both sensed and acknowledged one another.

Hearing the explosion, followed by the sound of raining debris downstairs echo through the open doorway of the attic, Johdi and Aaron's attention was suddenly shifted.

"What the hell was that?" startled, she queried.

Closing the book and dismissing the page and its contents, – something that risked exposing Rasima as she possessed Aaron's body – Johdi stepped away and began to cross the room. Moving forward, Aaron began to approach the book only to suddenly hit an invisible wall of energy that caused the book to give off a subtle green aura. Oblivious, Johdi had stood with her back to the exploit. Overpowering the magic, Aaron pushed through the protective magic of the book.

Speaking in Latin, she cast a spell, "Hidden from sight in still of night, disillusion this illusion, and obliterate this prison state." And with a brisk flick of her hands she used her own power of Energy Manipulation to create a small blast. "Hello, Husband." She made half a smile as she saw him sitting on the lounge room floor with Pridham beside him.

~*~

The golden light of the attic swooned around Aaron as he came close to the family's Book of Shadows on its stand. His amber colored eyes hungered for the power as the pupil dilated to the entirety of his eyes. Stepping around the stand, he halted and his eyes returned to normal. Aaron stood there staring hungrily at the green, leather bound object of immense power.

Sensing something unusual behind her, Johdi, with her back to her cousin as she observed the open attic door glanced out of the corner of her eye. Turning around slowly she witnessed Aaron's odd behavior.

"What are you doing?" she queried.

Promptly looking up and across at his cousin, Aaron extended his arm and fired a bolt of electricity. Swift to defend herself; Johdi's magic countered the demonic attack. The bolt of electricity hit a glimmering barrier of red energy as the witch mentally wielded her power of Petrifaction.

Aaron lowered his hand, deactivating his power, "Oops. I've been found out."

"Who the hell are you?" she growled, her glimmering protective shield vanished. "Aaron does not possess any magic, he gave it up."

Bursting in through the doorway, squawking crows filled the room and a startled Johdi dropped to the floor. Raising his hand as the murder came at him; Aaron destroyed the birds, burning up as they flew into a wall of invisible, heated energy.

Helped up to her feet by Noah, Johdi looked at her cousin with a look of comfort. Glancing past him, she witnessed Connemara step out of his shadow. Together, the three witches glared across the room at Aaron as he lowered his hand back to his side.

"And to think," Aaron spoke arrogantly as he smirked at his brother, sister-in-law and cousin, "how many failed attempts evil has made to snatch your fricken book of magic. Yet, here I am," magically his appearance altered and Rasima resumed her beautiful form, "succeeding everyone whoever came before me."

Placing her hands on the book, it did not repel her like it did before. She lifted it up into her arms and made an evil grin.

"Rafaela is dead," she revealed egotistically. "Asmodeus rules now. And you, Noah Pogue, along with your brother's shall burn–"

Outside, from the view of the street, an explosion blew out the windows and flames quickly took hold.

~*~

*I*n the darkened bedroom of his childhood home, lit only by the moonlight shining in through the space between the parted curtains, Perry gasped as he sat up in his bed as a child. Cold sweat drenched his hair and glittered across his forehead.

"Hello sweet boy," said a gentle, woman's voice at the foot of the bed. "Don't be afraid, I am an angel, sent by a higher power."

Stepping into the moonlight that covered the bed, Alera revealed herself. A tall, slender woman with long, flowing black hair was dressed in a maroon-colored batwing dress with a black belt around her waist.

"I know who you are." In his bed, Perry had resumed his adult form, "Alera."

She smirked at him, "You're an idiot to think you can stop me. Or the great evil of the Disciples or the Potentate." Her eyes filled with black and her voice deepened with demonic power, ***"TREADWELL IS OURS."***

Social Links

Website - http://www.trkester.com.au/

Instagram - https://www.instagram.com/t.r.kester/

Facebook - https://www.facebook.com/TRKesterBooks/

About the Author

I hail from Adelaide, South Australia, home of the renowned Barossa Valley and McLaren Vale Wines.

My humble city is also the murder capital of Australia.

I love all things fantasy. As a child, I loved writing short stories, but a passion for writing manifested at a turbulent point in my adolescence. My imagination has me away with the fairies most of the time, wishing I had a super power to triumph over all that is bad in this world. Reality has me working a nine-to-five job.

When I'm away from the computer, I love watching anime, drinking coffee to my heart's content, listening and dancing, around the house to music. I'm a child of the 80's nothing gets my imagination flowing like Bon Jovi.

I believe everyone has a book inside them, it just requires something to bring it to the surface.

www.ingramcontent.com/pod-product-compliance
Lightning Source LLC
Chambersburg PA
CBHW070957120726
47910CB00004B/1282